The Witching Well

S.D. Hintz

A
Grinning Skull Press
Publication

DEDICATION

To Ashanti,
Wife, soul mate, loving supporter

CONTENTS

ACKNOWLEDGMENTS

A huge thanks to Grinning Skull Press for metamorphosing this novel from a fuzzy caterpillar to a beautiful butterfly. I appreciate your passion for my work.

S.D.

Chapter 1

After I slit your mommy's throat, I'm gonna cut her face off.

Murray blocked the image before it could drown him. A month of therapy only made the memories more vivid, every session reliving the nightmare. While wounds healed, scars remained. Maybe, with time, the mental preoccupation would fade. He doubted it. Relocating to his grandmother's home—courtesy of his mother's will—would surely be a constant reminder.

He gazed out the passenger side window, straining to distract his thoughts. Towering firs swayed in a green blur. Churches and bars vied for the locals' devotion. Rustic inns lured travelers every other mile. The surroundings gave Murray an eerie vibe. Suburbia had been his comfort zone. Now, smack dab in the middle of bear country, he hoped Grandma Anna's car ran like new.

He squinted through the windshield as the forest thinned out and four-foot crags lined the roadside. Dogwoods and spruces edged the limestone, providing glimpses of a glistening Lake Superior between branches. They neared a timbered sign posted in a bed of violets and cyclamen, perhaps twenty yards beyond a scenic outlook.

**Welcome to
Windom
"Port of the North Shore"
Population 79**

Murray frowned. "Twenty more than Rushford."

Flashbacks of his hometown blinded him. His mom's flower shop, Roses in Rushford. Trading comic books with his best friend, Gilby Wells. Shooting hoops at Eden Elementary. Saturday spaghetti dinners at Lon's Diner. The Saturday dinner his mom canceled. That was the last time he saw her. The last time he held her. The last time...

He fought off the memory.

Grandma Anna smiled. "And just about a three-hour drive on the nose. To think, I left here yesterday morning. It feels like I've been gone for weeks."

For Murray, the previous two days had passed in slow motion. He thought back on the wake, the funeral, and the reluctant goodbyes. At the time, they seemed never-ending. Part of him had been eager for it all to end, while the other part refused to let go.

Tears welled up as he recalled his mom's casket being carried to the cemetery.

He wept for everyone and everything he left behind. His mom. His friends. His old life.

Grandma Anna squeezed his shoulder. "It's going to be

okay. I know it's hard right now, but we'll get through this together."

Murray dried his eyes and nodded. His grandmother's words dissolved in his tunnel vision. The setbacks seemed endless, seemed to bear down like an avalanche.

Grandma Anna decelerated as the Crown Victoria entered town, and seconds later she steered the car into a neighborhood. An odd development of multiple builders on different deadlines, it reminded Murray of Minneapolis; no two houses were alike. The car paused at an uncontrolled intersection. An olive street sign boasted Blossom Boulevard with the crossroad Philodendron Drive.

Murray stared out the window as they headed down the boulevard. He had never seen a more manicured block. On the left corner, a white picket fence encircled a quaint two-story house of the same hue, the lawn lime green and trimmed. A snaking row of flowering blackthorns coiled around back. A miniature picket fence edged a garden of sunflowers and lemon tulips. Welcome to Mr. Rogers' house.

Grandma Anna noticed Murray's interest. "That's Missus Muldoon's place. She tends her garden at nine o'clock sharp every day. It's her pride and joy. I wouldn't be surprised if it was surrounded by landmines."

"That's some hobby." Murray eyed the cantilever roof that extended from the front steps to the driveway. "How come she doesn't have a garage?"

"I guess she doesn't really need one. She rarely drives as it is. Probably why she's still alive and kicking."

"Weird."

"One thing's for sure, I don't go out of my way to talk to her, and neither should you. She's quite the oddball when she's not gardening. And I don't think she fancies children. I see her tear up those Pro-Life pamphlets all the time."

"Guess I'll keep my distance then."

Murray regarded the house on his right. Three stories of steel gray shutters and navy blue siding. Two twisted yew trees littered the lawn with blood-red cones and needles. The place looked haunted. An elderly woman stood in the broad bay window like a mannequin in a store display, staring at them as they passed by.

The thought of an old lady creeping in the curtains gave Murray the willies. "Who's that?"

Grandma Anna turned her head as if knowing precisely where to train her gaze. "That's Missus Vitikin. She's the town busybody." She paused and waved. "She loves to gossip, spread rumors, throw everyone under the bus. I do my best to keep the peace with her."

Paranoia seized Murray. "Does she know I'm coming?"

"Of course. She's my next-door neighbor. We talk every day, sometimes even have tea together. Well… This is it."

"*That's your house?*"

"*Our* house."

The four-story, rose-colored Victorian towered over the block. Red brick outlined the numerous windows and oak front door. Red and white roses graced the walk that stretched from the driveway to the front steps, which then wound a-round the side of the house through a vine-covered pergola. Blooming annuals encircled the trio of maple trees in the lush yard.

Murray gaped at the thought of relocating from a two-bedroom rambler to a mini-mansion. Maybe his new life wouldn't be so bad after all.

Grandma Anna parked the car, popped the trunk, and opened her door. "Let's grab your belongings. Then I'll give you a guided tour of the Macabe Place."

Murray unbuckled his seat belt. He gazed at the looming house. The Macabe Place. It sounded like a horror movie. It would surely haunt him with memories of his mom. He hoped the pain would pass with time, as his therapist implied. His suggestion of distracting the mind with work or a project possibly held weight and needed consideration.

Murray climbed out of the car and stretched. Standing never felt so good after sitting down for the last three hours. The warm breeze smelled of roses and freshly mowed grass. Again, he regarded the house. The sun peered over the left chimney and cast a glow on the third-story rose window. The whole setting possessed a refreshing air. Murray felt the vague sense of being on vacation at an extravagant bed and breakfast, which were more common than McDonald's in northern Minnesota.

He turned and headed to the rear of the car. His gaze drifted across the boulevard. An old, bald black man with wire-rimmed glasses casually approached the drive. He sported an electric blue suit and cream shirt with a cornflower bow tie. His black loafers glared more than his head. His greeting came with a deep voice.

"Need a hand, Anna?"

"Oh, hello, Cab. No, thank you. I think I can manage to carry one duffel bag."

"One duffel bag? Boy, if you plan on visitin' longer than the summer, my name's Cabot Linlith. My friends call me Cab; my neighbors call me Trouble."

He offered his hand. Murray gladly accepted it. "Murray."

Cab's handshake was firm, trusting. His hazel eyes twinkled. "Welcome to Windom. If you like shootin' the bull on the porch with raspberry lemonade, then I'm the man to see."

Murray grinned. "I'll see you soon then."

Grandma Anna shut the trunk. "After lunch." She pointed at Cab. "And you, young man, either forgot that Mass was yesterday or you have a hot date."

Cab bared a toothless smile. "Only with the sunshine, Anna. And Murray, if that's alright with you."

"Of course, but promise me you won't be gambling."

"Gamblin'? Why? 'Cause I'm on my way to church? No, ma'am. It's not bingo night. I made a deal with the Devil. I've got to help Reverend Regent with the potluck."

"Altar boy wasn't good enough?"

"He said I was too old. Imagine that." Cab shook his head. "Now if you'll excuse me, one can't be late with the Lord."

He waved and crossed the boulevard to his bronze Cadillac. Murray's anxiety eased. He dreaded the neighbors, especially after Grandma Anna's details concerning Mrs. Vitikin and Mrs. Muldoon. He knew the challenge of meeting new people, but what worried him most was befriending elderly adults. They always seemed so grumpy and needy. After encountering Cab, though, he wondered if he was being too judgmental, a quality he undoubtedly inherited from his mom.

Grandma Anna gestured toward the front steps. "Shall we?"

Murray nodded and followed her up the brick path. She stopped on the steps and unlocked the door, the brass knocker rattling against the solid oak.

Murray's eyes widened and lips parted. They stood in a large foyer, the floor hardwood and glossy, casting a mirror reflection. Oil paintings of bouquets and gardens decorated the apricot walls. A set of marble benches flanked a glass end table with a crystal vase of red roses set upon it. A sweeping oak stairway disappeared above.

Grandma Anna slipped off her black pumps. "You can set your shoes by the door for now. Your bedroom's upstairs. I think we'll head up there, and you can take some time to unpack your things. Once you've made yourself at home, I'll give you the grand tour."

"Okay."

Murray tailed Grandma Anna up the staircase, each step creaking. He could not wait to see his new bedroom. The thought of decorating it from scratch with comic book and movie posters excited him. He could even paint the walls if Grandma Anna allowed him the privilege. He had yet to test the boundaries of their relationship, but that would come in time.

An open landing of hardwood floors extended from the top of the stairs. More oil paintings of annuals covered the walls. To the left, a wrought-iron spiral staircase led to the third story. Grandma Anna headed right down a wide hall-way of four propped-open doors.

Her voice echoed down the hall. "The first room on the right is the bathroom. The other three are bedrooms. The last one on the left is yours. The one across the way was your aunt's and mother's."

"They shared a room?"

"'Til your mother was sixteen. Aunt Eva was five years older and out of the house by twenty-one. Speaking of which, she'll be stopping by tomorrow with a few things of your mother's." Grandma Anna sighed as she set down the duf-fel bag. "Well, here it is. It should do for now. It used to be your Grandpa Macon's study. The bed was your mother's."

Murray stepped inside. "Thank you."

"You're welcome. I'll let you unpack."

Grandma Anna left Murray to absorb the spacious room. Sunlight poured through the two double-paned win-dows, casting a glare on the floor. A pair of bookcases leaned against the far wall, plumb full of paperbacks and hardcovers. On the right sat an oak dresser with a large globe and match-ing roll-top desk. All remnants of the converted study.

Murray's eyes locked on the four-poster. Hand-carved across the headboard, roses intertwined a thorny vine. Grand-ma Anna had removed the canopy, surely so it looked less feminine, but the white lace comforter remained. Murray fought the urge to lie down and test the mattress. After the long car ride, an intended catnap would have him waking up at bedtime.

He unzipped his duffel bag and sifted through the contents. He filled the top dresser drawer with tube socks and briefs, the middle with his iron-on T-shirts, and the bottom with his Marvel comic book collection. He piled his folded pants and jean shorts on the desk, lacking the energy to hang them in the closet.

He shoved the duffel bag beneath the bed and plopped down on the comforter. He stared at the ceiling, his mind eagerly drifting. He wondered how many times his mom had lain in the same bed lost in thought. Certainly hundreds, if not thousands of nights. Had she ever felt alone, a young girl in a little bed against the entire world? Murray failed to ignore the feeling as it crept over him like a translucent body bag. Of course, Grandma Anna raised her through childhood. Motherless, he had…Grandma Anna. He closed his heavy eyelids and felt his mind running off without him. The ceiling turned to sky, and the comforter became a cloud. His room of loneliness filled with imaginary friends, and he embraced it wholeheartedly.

Chapter 2

"Murray, Murray. What's your hurry? You've got no-where to run."

Clouded shards of memories flooded Murray like a deluge. His mom waving goodbye on the doorstep before walking to her killer's black sedan. The doorbell awakening Murray on the living room couch. The sheriff delivering the news and escorting him to the car. Sobbing in the backseat. Waiting at the police station for his best friend's parents, hugging his knees to his chest. Standing beside his mom's closed coffin, wishing he could see her one last time.

Murray forced his eyes open. He glanced from wall to wall. For a moment, he thought he was in his bedroom at Rushford. The decor of garden paintings brought him back full circle. He dozed off on his mom's four-poster.

Movement caught his eye. Grandma Anna stood to his right with her back turned. She placed a small brass lamp on the desk. Murray sat up and rubbed his eyes.

Grandma Anna turned at the squeak of bed springs. "Up so soon? You only napped for a half-hour."

"Had a bad dream. I can't… I can't stop thinking about

him. I see him every time I close my eyes."

Grandma Anna touched Murray's cheek lovingly. "You think you see him. Maybe you even want to see him. But you'll never see him here. He's buried far away at that."

Murray looked down at the satin sheets, the daymare still haunting him.

Grandma Anna hugged him tight and kissed him on the forehead. "You're in Windom now. No one's coming to get you. I won't let them. You're safe here."

Murray nodded as he met Grandma Anna's aquamarine eyes; they twinkled like gemstones, as his mom's had.

"So, Mister Macabe, would you like to help me with my garden? The fresh air might do you some good."

Murray sighed, still rattled. "I think I'd rather stay inside."

"Indoors it is. How about a tour of the attic instead? That's where I usually go when I need some time to myself."

"Okay. Sure."

Murray sidled out of bed and followed Grandma Anna into the hallway. He noticed she changed out of her dress into more casual apparel, salmon slacks, and a cream blouse. Her perfume wafted as she walked, smelling of roses and lilacs. She crossed the landing and ascended the spiral staircase.

Murray's overactive imagination took hold. Butterflies fluttered in his belly. He wondered what Grandma Anna had in store. Thanks to films like *The Changeling* and *Flowers in the Attic,* he always considered the top floor the creepiest room in a house. At the same time, he expected it to be a dusty disaster area, cluttered wall to wall with antique junk and family heirlooms. His heart thumped with every step. The staircase wobbled under their weight, unaccustomed to supporting two people.

Grandma Anna paused, regarded Murray, and then pointed over her shoulder. "When this door is closed, that means I want to be alone. No disruptions whatsoever."

Murray nodded with a furrowed brow. He bit his tongue as thoughts of Grandma Anna's private goings-on prodded him.

She noted his confusion and added quickly, "When it's open, you can come up here whenever you like. Understand?"

"Yeah."

"Good."

Grandma Anna turned and lifted the trap door. It creaked like a sealed coffin. She ascended the last few steps. Murray anxiously followed in her shadow. The moment he entered the room, sunlight blinded him, and a hint of incense smothered his sense of smell.

Taken aback, he scanned the attic, turning on his heels to take it all in. It exceeded his expectations. By far the largest room in the house, vaulted ceilings and double-paned windows eased the need for artificial light. The hardwood floor gleamed as if recently varnished, sparkling with a green and red kaleidoscopic reflection from the rose window above. Oil paintings of blooming flowers and majestic gardens decorated what little wall space existed.

Murray's gaze locked on the left side of the room, and his eyes widened. Before the corner window sat a blue easel and gray tray of paints, from which jutted a wood stool. A semi-circle of five red candelabras created a boundary line. A crystal chandelier dangled from the ceiling, surely spotlighting the space at nightfall. Murray suddenly felt the urge to paint, like back in middle school art class.

Grandma Anna withdrew a black matchbook from her pant's pocket. "This side of the room I call my gallery. This is where I spend most of my time thinking—and painting."

Murray approached a framed landscape of a field of daisies receding into a glimmering pond hanging between two windows. "Wow. These paintings are really good. Do you ever sell any of them?"

"Sometimes. A little extra spending money never hurts."

"You must be up here a lot then."

"That's not the only thing I do for a living, sweetie." Grandma Anna struck the match and began lighting the candelabra. "I used to be a registered nurse. I volunteer at the nursing home twice a week. It gets me out of the house."

Murray noted the right side of the attic. A black curtain undulated from the rafters, concealing the corner and a quarter of the room.

Murray pointed. "What's behind the curtain?"

Grandma Anna glanced at it and flashed him a stern gaze. "That's my dark room. I devote a good chunk of time to it. It is also the only room in the house you are forbidden to go. Your mother learned the hard way. I trust you'll respect my wishes."

Murray nodded reluctantly, taken aback, as Grandma Anna lit the last candelabrum.

She blew out the match and set it on the paint tray. "Now if you'll excuse me, I need to water my garden. If you'd like to test out the canvas, be my guest. I set out some fresh watercolors earlier. And believe me, painting is a nice way to clear your mind. I've found it's the best way to pour out all the feelings I bottle up inside."

"Maybe I'll give it a try."

"You do that. I'll come back up in a little while to see your masterpiece."

Murray smiled, and Grandma Anna disappeared downstairs. Seconds later, his curiosity wandered back to the black curtain.

What was the big secret? Was she hiding something illegal back there?

Whatever it concealed, his mother had known at one

time. But only once from the sound of it. Grandma Anna had surely punished her for snooping. And truth be told, he wanted to avoid her mean streak. Like many adults, she probably detonated when you pushed her buttons.

A loud slam made Murray jump. He whirled. The trapdoor shut on its own. He looked to the windows facing the boulevard. The maroon draperies billowed in the wind, caught red-handed. He approached them and shut the window part way, paranoid the fiery candelabra might blow over next. He'd rather not burn down Grandma Anna's favorite room.

His eyes zoomed in on the easel. The blue paint flaked around the edges and fluttered in the breeze. Besides the obvious wear and tear, it otherwise appeared to be in solid condition. Years ago he painted on one. Back then he had to wear a smock and hairnet and use one of those fat brushes. Now he could paint in his regular clothes and create whatever he desired.

He rounded the candelabra, savoring the heavenly scent of cinnamon. Just as Grandma Anna said, a blank canvas awaited with a tray of fresh paints. He pulled out the oak stool and sat down, the legs creaking beneath his weight. He picked up a slender brush and scanned the watercolors. The circle of red paint glinted in the sunlight.

The color of choice. The heart of his anger and pain.

Red.

Blood red.

Murray plunged the brush into the open wound. Instantaneously, his heart bled through his fingers. His strokes slashed at the canvas like a knife. Red splattered and trickled, trailing onto the easel. His eyes welled up as his emotions took hold.

Concocted images of his mother assaulted him. Her face contorted as she struggled in a chokehold. Wailing with each stab wound in an alley on her knees. Her bloody hand reaching desperately over the lip of a dumpster.

A whimper escaped Murray's throat. His breathing became more labored with each lash. Tears spilled down his cheeks, splashing in the watercolors like a blood rain. The brush shook in his fingers, reluctant to stab again. It slipped from his grip and clanged on the tray.

Murray's shoulders slumped, and his head hung low as he sobbed uncontrollably in the afternoon sunlight.

The trapdoor creaked open.

Grandma Anna entered the attic. "So, how's the Picasso coming?"

Unresponsive, Murray clutched the stool to keep his weary body from falling off. He stared straight ahead, his focus drowning in the watercolors. His lip trembled, struggling to form a word. He wiped his tear-stained cheeks with the back of his hand.

Grandma Anna placed her hands on his shoulders. "It's been how long since you last painted?"

Murray shrugged, cleared his throat. "I… I don't know." He looked up into Grandma Anna's smiling face. "You were right. I feel…"

"Relieved?"

Murray thought momentarily, then nodded. "Yeah, relieved. It felt good…to get that all out."

"It always does. Never hold back your feelings. Not only will they eat you alive, but they'll hurt the loved ones around you." Grandma Anna squeezed his arms. "Now tell me all about your painting."

"I… I don't know how to explain it."

"Is that blood everywhere?"

"Yeah."

"And that's his car?"

Murray nodded.

"So why is it so sunny?"

Murray regarded the giant yellow star in the cloudless sky. "Because…there's hope…somewhere after this."

Grandma Anna hugged him and kissed his cheek. "Well done. Now, all we need is a place to hang it."

Murray spoke his mind before he could bite his tongue. "How about in the dark room?"

Grandma Anna shared his haunted gaze. "But you'll never see it in there."

Murray shrugged.

Grandma Anna stared at the curtain. "That sounds like the perfect place." She rounded the candelabra and blew them out one by one. "Now go wash up. You look like you've been finger painting. I'll cook an early dinner at three since we didn't eat anything on the road. Hopefully, you'll find your appetite by then."

A grin cracked Murray's frown. "As long as it's not tuna casserole."

Grandma Anna raised her thin, silver brows. "Your mother learned that dish from me. It was one of her favorites. Consider yourself lucky."

With that, she chuckled and left the attic. Murray eyed his artwork one last time. He decided whatever he painted in the attic would remain there. The room possessed a special spirit. A means of therapy, a shoulder to cry on. It provided privacy and an outlet to let emotions run free. All the sunlight and shadows—windows to the soul. Whether Murray wanted to admit or not, the attic had seized him in its clutches.

He stood and pushed the stool under the easel. He regarded the dark room one last time. The curtain fluttered like a vampire's cape; the shadows wavered, teasing the sunlight. A ghost of a smile haunted Murray's face. Deep down he knew he shared more in common with Grandma Anna than a child should. He hoped it meant their relationship would grow stronger. At this point, Grandma Anna was all he had.

The telephone rang as Murray took his seat at the dining room table. Grandma Anna cut it short and snatched up the receiver.

Murray's eyes wandered around the dining room. French doors separated it from the living room. Two opposite paintings decorated the oak-paneled walls: one of a rose on a brick doorstep, the other a flowery pergola with a sunset backdrop. A crystal chandelier sparkled above the set table; the fine china and silverware gleamed in its bright glow. In the center of the lace tablecloth stood a white ceramic vase of pink roses.

Murray analyzed the aroma wafting from the kitchen. It smelled delicious, like Alfredo, definitely not the stench of tuna casserole.

The French doors slid open. Grandma Anna strolled in with a silver platter of fettuccine garnished with basil and lightly toasted garlic bread.

She set the food on the table. "That was your Aunt Eva on the phone. She's stopping by tomorrow with those things of your mother's."

Murray's eyebrows arched. "Like what?"

"She didn't say. She did, however, mention that she's been meaning to talk to you."

"About what?"

"She didn't say that either." Grandma Anna sat across from Murray and unfolded her napkin. "I do know she's hurting right now. Your mother was her only sister. Her best friend." She paused as she composed herself. She raised her napkin and dabbed a tear that threatened to fall. "She hardly ever comes up here to see me, you know? Once a year, if I'm lucky. I talk to her on the phone, of course, but…it's not quite the same. It doesn't help she lives three hours away."

As Grandma Anna dished out their dinner, Murray considered her comment. The extent of his mom's death sank in. Aunt Eva truly suffered. After all, she and his mom ran the flower shop together, working with each other on a daily basis. Best friends indeed.

Grandma Anna hurt even more. Murray noticed every time she mentioned his mom. He assumed since she was older she'd dealt with the passing easier. Unlike in his case, thirteen years old, losing the only person who loved him.

"Grandma? Why did my mom leave here?"

Grandma Anna ate a forkful of pasta, swallowing it before meeting Murray's gaze. "Did she ever talk about growing up in this town?"

Murray shook his head. "Not really."

"Well, she was a bit of a homebody, didn't have a lot of friends. But then again, there's always been a lack of children in Windom."

Murray's serving of noodles froze before his mouth. "Are there kids here now?"

"Not in this neighborhood, at least not that I'm aware of. Mister Linlith and Missus Vitikin have children and grandchildren, they just don't visit much. And trust me, I know how that is."

Murray's paranoia devoured his appetite. He couldn't possibly be the only kid in town. If true, what would he do with himself? No friends, no playmates. He would die of boredom!

He lowered his fork to the plate. "Where's the school at?"

"About twenty miles from here in Highland, same place your mother attended. That, in itself, made most of her friendships long distance. Even so, as she got older, she seemed more restless, more eager to get away."

"Get away? From who?"

"Oh… Everybody. Me. Grandpa Macon. Windom."

"But why? I don't get it."

Grandma Anna raised her wineglass and sipped. "When your Aunt Eva left, that was inspiration enough. Your mother… Well, that's a day I'll never forget."

Murray's throat was parched, as if thirsting for the knowledge his mom kept secret. He grabbed his tumbler of water and took a gulp. He looked down at his plate.

"What happened?"

Grandma Anna eyed Murray, her jaw stiffening, clearly reluctant to share the information. After a five-second silence, she decided otherwise.

"She came home that night after seeing a movie and… and told us she was four months pregnant. She had just graduated high school and didn't have a job, and…and we didn't know the boy she was dating. We never did meet him. We all got into a yelling match, which I now regret…" She sighed and drank her wine. "She skipped town the next day, and your Aunt Eva took her in."

The story spun through Murray's brain like a Tilt-A-Whirl. His mom left Windom because of him. He had dismantled the happy family. The thought rattled him.

"So my mom left because of me."

"No, no, honey, not at all. It wasn't because of you. Don't ever think that. There were plenty of other reasons. Plenty. As she got older, we all banged heads a lot more. Argued, disagreed. I suppose I tried to control her too much. I just wanted what was best for her. And she—she wanted a life of her own."

"But why didn't my dad go with her?"

"She never told you that either?"

Murray shook his head. He knew little about his dad. His mom once said: "He's not here, that's all you need to know." Afterward, he avoided the matter. Obviously, the man disrespected her in some way. Her relationships seemed to bleed together. The last man… Murray simmered his bubbling anger and refocused on his original inquiry.

A flash of resentment passed over Grandma Anna's face. "Like the last man, he treated her like trash. When he found out she was pregnant, he gave her five dollars for diapers and bought a train ticket to Canada. That was the last we heard of him. I think that's what really made your mother want to get away from everything. Quite frankly, I never blamed her. I probably would have done the same."

Murray processed the information, letting his mind drift in retrospect. Reluctant to go out on dates, men approached his mom all the time. She typically declined, but over the years Murray could tell an umbrella of loneliness opened even on sunny days. She would often nurse a glass of wine in the late evening, embraced by the darkness of the living room, comforted by the murmuring television. He figured she eventually came to terms with herself and decided a kind man waited somewhere out there for her. If only she remained lonely, she would still be alive.

Grandma Anna noted the gloom in Murray's eyes. "Let's change the subject, shall we? How do you like my fettuccine?"

Murray stepped out of his mental closet and regarded his untouched plate. The noodles clumped on the fork. He brought the serving to his lips. "It's good. Tastes like a restaurant cooked it."

"Wait 'til you try my tuna casserole."

Murray grinned. "I think I'd rather have seconds."

"Already? Shouldn't you finish the firsts?"

Murray scooped up another forkful as his appetite returned with a vengeance. The tasty food also improved his mood. He washed down a bite and looked across the table. "Thanks for showing me the attic today."

Grandma Anna smiled. "You're welcome. What's mine is yours now, sweetie. You're not a guest. You're my grandson."

Chapter 3

Grandma Anna being a seasoned early bird, Murray turned in at eight o'clock and awoke around six the next morning feeling well rested. His mom's bed triumphed once again. He only wished it had the power to fend off the nightmares.

Fragments of dreams glimmered like lakeshore agates. His mom's killer revealing a meat cleaver from a bouquet of red roses. Murray running after the black sedan as his mom screamed for help. Cemetery workers shoveling dirt onto his mom's coffin six feet below.

Murray blinked his sleep-encrusted eyes and sighed. He wished the nightmares would end. They'd been haunting him every night since his mom's death. Would he ever sleep soundly again? He doubted it.

He peeked between the curtains beside the bed.

The sun blazed on the pink horizon in a cloudless sky. Another beautiful day in Windom. Murray thought about the sparkling blue waters of Lake Superior. He hoped some time soon he would be able to stroll the boardwalk. Probably not today, though. He recalled Aunt Eva was stopping by, so surely Grandma Anna had cleared her schedule.

She has a few things for you that belonged to your mother.

Murray wondered what they could be. Photos? One of her cherished vases? A piece of jewelry? Hopefully, not a knickknack stashed away in a bottom drawer. A tinge of selfishness prodded him. When he left the house in Rushford, he forgot about his mom's belongings. He crossed his fingers and hoped Aunt Eva assumed the responsibility.

He climbed out of bed and sifted through the dresser drawers. He dug out a pair of khaki shorts and a blue Ocean Pacific T-shirt. He dressed quickly, eager to enjoy the day's pleasant weather. He tossed his dirty clothes aside, made the bed, then hurried out of the bedroom.

He paused at the top of the staircase. His stomach growled at the scent of bacon and toast. He tramped down the steps and headed into the kitchen.

Grandma Anna turned from the window with a cup of tea in hand. Dressed in a pair of cream slacks and a white blouse, she had even done her hair up in a bun. She smiled warmly. "Good morning. Sleep well?"

"Very."

"Good. How were the dreams?"

Murray shrugged. "The same."

Grandma Anna nodded and set her cup down on the mahogany table. At the lone place setting, she proceeded to heap the plate with scrambled eggs, bacon, and two slices of toast. "Have a seat. I thought a hearty breakfast might brighten your morning."

"Oh yeah! This is way better than a Pop-Tart."

"And more nutritious. There's a ton more energy in home cooking than a toaster treat. Maybe one of these mornings we'll stop by Kay's Cafe. They have some of the best boysenberry waffles this side of the lake."

The phone rang, halting their chitchat.

Grandma Anna headed to the living room. "That could

only be one person calling at this hour."

Murray looked out the bay window as he ate a bacon strip. Across the street, Cab sat on his porch with a newspaper in hand. He took a sip of his orange juice and looked up. He smiled and toasted his glass. Murray grinned and did the same.

Oddly, he felt like he was being watched. And most of the houses seemed to face window to window. He certainly didn't need an audience seeing him undress in his bedroom.

Grandma Anna returned, shaking her head. "That was Missus Vitikin. She cooks more than Betty Crocker. That's the third time this week she's asked me for an ingredient. One of these days I'm going to tell her I'm out just to see her walk down to the market."

She reached across the counter for her spice rack and spun it. She removed a glass bottle of dark green herb.

Murray furrowed his brow. "Does she call you a lot?"

"She's a lonely old lady, Murray. I've learned to live with it. I'll be back before you can ask for seconds."

Grandma Anna strolled out of the kitchen. Moments later, the front door clicked shut. Murray watched Grandma Anna pass by the bay window. Across the street, Cab looked up from his newspaper. He shook his head and set his empty glass on the porch rail.

The phone rang.

Murray jumped out of his seat, startled. He wondered if he should answer it. A crazy thought urged otherwise. What if Mrs. Vitikin was calling to talk to him? She knew Grandma Anna was out of the house. It would be the perfect opportunity.

The phone rang again. Murray stood up from the table. Could the call be important? After all, he lived here now; wasn't he obligated to answer the phone and take a message?

A third ring resounded from the living room. Murray

shook off his paranoia and hurried out of the kitchen.

"Hello?"

"Hello? Who is this? Murray? Murray, is that you?"

Murray sighed. It was only Aunt Eva. "Yeah."

"Where's your grandmother?"

"Next door."

"Next door? At Missus Vitikin's?"

"Yeah."

"Can you tell her that I'm leaving Rushford around eight? I should be at Windom by noon."

"Okay."

"Sugar? How are you? How is everyone treating you there?"

"So far so good."

"Well, don't worry. Things will work out. I collected some of your mother's stuff the other day at the house. I have something of hers that I'm sure she'd want you to have. So I'll see you soon, dear."

"Bye, Aunt Eva."

"Bye."

Murray hung up the phone and turned the conversation over in his head. His eyes glazed. He saw his house in Rushford, an empty skeleton picked apart by vultures. A real estate agent had posted a "For Sale" sign in the rosebushes. Moving vans lined up along the curb. News reporters lingered at the end of the drive near yellow tape.

Murray blinked away the images. No longer home, it burned a temperate memory, a place of happy and sad recollections.

The guessing game commenced. Something of his mom's... What could it be? A photo album? A perfume bottle? Her music box?

Grandma Anna passed by the bay window. Moments later, the front door opened as Murray sat down at the kitchen table. He shoved the last forkful of eggs into his mouth.

Grandma Anna entered the kitchen, smiling at Murray's clean plate. "I bet you were just about to ask for seconds."

Murray drained his orange juice. "No thanks. I'm full." He wiped his mouth with his napkin. He paused briefly, hoping Grandma Anna wouldn't be upset with him for answering the phone. "Aunt Eva called while you were gone. She said she'd be here by noon."

"Splendid. The three of us can lunch together."

Murray nodded, crumpled his napkin. "So what's Missus Vitikin cooking?"

"You know, I asked her that same question. She said she's pickling beets."

"Beets?"

"Yep. Knowing her, she'll probably make a sandwich out of it."

The idea of an old woman eating beets soured Murray's stomach. He could feel his eggs scrambling up his throat. "Did she say anything about me?"

Grandma Anna's crow's feet deepened. "What would she have to say about you? She hasn't even met you yet."

Murray shrugged and averted his gaze to the window.

"Missus Vitikin may be nosy, but she's just lonely. She loves soap operas, drama, solving mysteries." Grandma Anna paused. "Murray, all of the neighbors know who you are and why you're here. It's no secret."

Murray looked down at the table sheepishly. Of course, everyone knew. In small towns, word traveled lightning fast. Once again, he jumped to conclusions. He hated being the new kid on the block. He felt as if he was under surveillance, like the slightest move would spark the neighbors to pour out of their houses for a look-see. For the record, Cab had watched him from his porch while he ate breakfast, which gave some support to the theory.

Grandma Anna leaned across the table. "Give her a chance. She's a quirky woman, but I'm sure you'll warm up to her."

Murray looked back out the window at the deserted boulevard. Cab's newspaper fluttered on the vacant porch. Mrs. Muldoon's sunflowers swayed metronomically, as if trying to peak around the tulips for a glimpse. Mrs. Muldoon herself…lingered near the blackthorns…staring straight at him!

Murray's jaw dropped, and he turned to voice his concern.

Grandma Anna left the table and headed for the doorway. "Rinse your dishes off and meet me in the backyard. I could use your help with the garden."

Murray stood too quickly, nudging the table with his midsection, rattling the place setting. He couldn't wait to escape the kitchen's display window.

Murray stepped outside onto the red brick patio and squinted at his surroundings. The far right corner housed a large bed of blooming red and white roses ranging from two to four feet in height. They'd been landscaped with mulch and mossy stones the size of grapefruits. A windy gravel path branched off from the patio and disappeared into the garden. To the left, a stone birdbath wobbled beneath a towering maple, occupied by two crows pecking at the basin puddle of two-day-old rain.

Grandma Anna appeared from around the side of the house, uncoiling a green hose into the yard. "Well, that's my rose garden. They're probably dying of thirst. Come along."

Murray followed her as she dragged the hose to the edge of the garden.

She knelt and began studying all of the rose petals, pinpointing the parched and wilted. "Gertrude Stein once said 'A rose is a rose is a rose.'"

"What's that mean?"

"To most people, it means 'things are what they are,' you know, 'it is what it is.' In Stein's poem, it's a lot deeper than that. Now, with this garden, I can water and prune it to death, but it still comes down to the soil and the roots. Although I can't stand the thought of just watching them wilt away."

Grandma Anna paused and slipped on a pair of white gardening gloves. "Do you like to read, Murray?"

"Yeah. Mostly comic books. It feels more like I'm watching a movie then."

"Ahhh, I see. Any particular ones?"

"The Punisher, Dr. Doom, Iron Fist, all the Marvel stuff."

"They sound very—foreboding."

"Nah, they're pretty fun."

Murray scanned the flowers. Grandma Anna invested countless hours in the garden. Each row alternated from red to white. Each plant was spaced identically, as if the distance had been measured with a ruler.

Grandma stood with a slight groan. "Murray? Would you be a dear and go turn on the hose for me? The spigot's on the side of the house, just off the path."

"Okay."

"Thank you, sweetie."

Murray turned and headed toward the path winding to the front yard. The roses flanked him momentarily, swaying, leaning after him. He stepped up his pace. He sighed as the garden receded like waves on a shore, the haunts failing to snag him in their undertow. He set foot on the sun-bleached bricks and hurried to the corner of the house.

The dreary neighboring dwelling came into view. A mighty oak cast the fenceless backyard in shadows. Dandelions and creeping Charlie dotted the ankle-high lawn. A rusted, chain link kennel begged for use beside an overgrown mulberry. The house itself was a two-story split-level with stucco walls and shuttered windows. The slate half-hip roof added to the overall resemblance of a giant tombstone. Murray figured it was either haunted or once served as a mortuary.

He spotted the white spigot protruding from the side of the house, fastened to the green hose. A trickle of water seeped from the connection and dripped below. Murray approached it and reached for the red handle.

A shadow flitted out of the corner of his eye. A guttural growl stopped him in his tracks, his hand frozen on the handle.

He turned his head and looked over his shoulder. A jet-black Rottweiler crept from the shadows of the yard. Murray's first thought was *Cujo*, even though the breed differed. It bared its fangs, snarling as it slunk between the oaks, pursuing its prey like a starved lion.

Murray's heart somersaulted, and his body broke into a sweat. He looked to his right. Grandma Anna remained in the backyard, out of sight.

He let go of the handle and backpedaled. He grunted as the spigot jabbed him in the calf. *Cornered!* His mind hurtled through corridors of past advice. He knew it wise to stand tall and allow a dog to sniff the hand. Yet with a hostile animal, did the same rules apply? He knew he could make a run for it, but doubted he would win the race.

The Rottweiler continued to approach, slowly stalking through the shadows. It crossed the property line, which was divided by a sunray. Its gaze narrowed, full of rage, as if the mere sight of a child ruined its day.

Murray glanced about, eyes wide, praying Grandma Anna would show up, perhaps wondering what delayed his return. No such luck.

The Rottweiler sprinted toward him, barking breathlessly. It stopped a yard away and snapped its jaws.

Murray cringed against the house. "Grandma!"

"Pontius! Heel! Heel!"

The Rottweiler froze, leering as drool oozed through its fangs. It snarled, yearning to disobey the gruff voice.

A pale old man with ashen hair emerged from the shadows. Dressed in a sweat-stained tank top and faded black slacks, he approached with a limp, hunched over, a cigar between clenched teeth. His bushy brows knitted and his sienna eyes burned. He paused at the property line and yanked the stogie from his mouth.

"You're Anna's boy, aren't you?"

Murray's heart pounded in his head. He hoped to God Grandma Anna had either heard his yell or the maniacal barking. "Yeah. Murray."

"*Anna's boy.*" The man stressed the two words as if it were an insult. He slapped his thigh, and the Rottweiler padded to his side, all the while keeping its eyes trained on Murray. "This here is Pontius. He hates children, as do I. So you stay the hell out of my yard!"

"I wasn't in your yard!"

"But when you are, you'll see how hard he bites!"

"Mister Havlock!"

Grandma Anna stormed around the corner, her fists clenched and her blue eyes blazing like a blowtorch.

Mr. Havlock seized Pontius by the collar and pulled him back. Glaring, they steeled themselves, as if both knew the impending danger of Hurricane Anna.

Grandma Anna reached across the property line and jabbed her index finger into Mr. Havlock's chest. "Keep that mutt away from my grandson! You hear me? This is your only warning."

"Then what?" Pontius growled with his master. "The threats start? No need. Anna's boy won't be nosing in my yard, will he?"

Grandma Anna dug her finger in like an awl. Her voice changed to cold and calm. "No one will be nosing in your yard, Mister Havlock. And your mutt better not be nosing around in my yard either. Now please go back to that hole you slithered from before I lose my temper."

Mr. Havlock's hand trembled as he placed the cigar back in his mouth. He puffed it and blew the smoke sideways, contemplating Grandma Anna's threat.

"Pontius! To heel!"

With that, mutt and master marched off into the shadows, grumbling and snarling.

Grandma Anna lifted Murray's chin. "How are you, honey?"

Murray regained his composure, willing his heartbeat to slow. He wiped the sweat from his brow. "Okay, I guess. What's his problem?"

"He's got a grudge with me, but that's no reason for him to sic his dog on you. He's just looking for another way to get under my skin."

"But why's he so mad?"

Grandma Anna lowered her voice, gazing at Mr. Havlock's yard. "Well, the other day he mowed down one of my rose beds, so I pruned the hell out of his maple tree. That one over there."

She pointed at his front yard. Murray turned his head. The maple looked winterkilled, leafless, the branches severed in half. Fall colors faded from its future. Murray regarded Grandma Anna with raised brows.

She met his look with the same cold glare. "Do me a

favor and stay clear of him. Understand? I don't dally with second warnings."

Murray nodded. After the recent run-in, he hesitated to challenge Grandma Anna's authority. That glimpse into her dark side spotlighted a place he knew rivaled hellfire.

Grandma Anna crossed over to the spigot and turned the handle. The hose wriggled like a snake as the water gushed forth. She nodded toward the backyard.

Murray tailed her down the path. His thoughts fixated on Pontius. Dogs terrified him, especially their unpredictability. "What if that dog comes after me again?"

"If that happens, you do what you just did. Call for help. That mutt's a menace." Grandma Anna headed for the garden. "Oh, that figures." She turned and looked down the length of the hose. "There must be a kink. I bet it's that darn spigot again."

She picked up the hose and yanked it, but it failed to spout water. She shook her head, dropped it, and looked at her dirty hands.

"Would you look at that? Murray, I need to go grab a rag. Would you be a dear again and run back to the spigot? That's usually where the kink is. And don't worry. Pontius is long gone. He's probably in the house by now. Just call me if you need me. I'll be back in a jiffy."

Murray nodded, and Grandma Anna left him standing there, staring at the corner of the house. Reluctantly, he headed back to the path. Hypothetical situations galore plagued him. What if Pontius lurked around the corner? Or what if Mr. Havlock hid in his backyard, itching to let him loose? Murray considered grabbing a stick for self-defense.

He traced his footsteps around the corner of the house. His pace slowed as he gauged Mr. Havlock's yard. The shadows wavered, reaching and retracting. The maple rustled, serving as nature's wind chime. Murray's eyes darted from tree to tree, searching for the slightest movement. Save for the light breeze, everything appeared still.

Taking no chances, Murray dashed to the spigot. Beneath the faucet, the hose was knotted like a pretzel. He crouched and quickly straightened out the kink. The water spurted down the length of the hose. Pleased with his handiwork, he stood and set his sights on the backyard.

"Where's your grandmother?"

Murray whirled and stumbled back against the side of the house. An old woman as tall as Grandma Anna had snuck up on him from the front yard. Her face of folds had survived many harsh winters and family funerals, her cheeks creased with wrinkles and spotted with liverworts. Her tight-lipped mouth was set like a bear trap while her eyes narrowed to slits. Her charcoal-gray curly hair could have been dyed in a chimney. She wore a black dress with a spiral pattern matching the cane she impatiently tapped on the ground.

The woman scowled. "Well? Speak up, boy! I know you can talk. The whole block just heard you mouth off."

Taken aback by her stern demeanor, Murray pointed down the path. "She's back there. By the garden."

"Of course she is."

The old woman hobbled around the corner, jabbing her cane in the grass like a ski pole.

Murray sighed. The morning excitement made him wish he was indoors. After a few moments of mental debate, he reluctantly returned to the backyard. As he rounded the house, he watched Grandma Anna emerge from the patio and head off the old woman.

"Eveleth? Thank God! For a second there I thought you were someone else. I assume you met my grandson, Murray?"

"Murray," the woman drawled. "Yes. He has Marilyn's eyes. Pity, isn't it?"

Grandma Anna gritted her teeth at the word "pity." "It is—nice to see her traits in him. Murray. This is Missus Vitikin."

Murray locked glares with their neighbor as he joined Grandma Anna's side. Saying "hello" was far from the tip of his tongue. He managed a slight nod.

Grandma Anna wiped her hands on the towel. "So, who's stirring the pot this morning?"

Mrs. Vitikin smirked, grounding her cane into the grass. "I think we both know the answer to that. Daisy just called and told me she saw Havlock come over here. She said Pontius was off his leash again. You know what happened the last time he was loose. Everyone's okay, I gather?"

Grandma Anna glanced at Murray. "Yes, thank you. I think Murray's a bit shaken, but he'll live. As for the next time I catch Havlock in my yard…"

"It's a long time coming. Daisy said he's been spending hours in his garage at night."

"And she's sure he hasn't just been keeping a light on?"

"Positive. She's seen sparks flying in the windows. Keep an eye on him, Anna. The toughest neighbors to watch are the ones next door."

"Eveleth, we both know I'm not one to play Peeping Tom. I leave that to you and Daisy."

"Well, you'd be wise to model our behavior. Do you really think Havlock is going to call a truce after you murdered his maple?"

"Oh no, I'm sure he'll retaliate. I just don't want Murray getting caught in the middle."

"You should've thought of that before you started a war with him. Heed my advice, Anna. You know I mean well."

Grandma Anna gazed at Havlock's yard, stone-faced. "I know. You're right. I need to keep my guard up."

An awkward silence fell. Murray shuffled his feet and

looked over his shoulder. After the exchange of gossip, which seemed relentless, he felt exposed, as if under a watchful eye. That thought alone made his skin crawl. And the talk of Mr. Havlock's plot of vengeance made him paranoid. He was a target, the easiest way to get back at Grandma Anna.

Mrs. Vitikin cleared her throat and removed her hand from the right pocket of her dress. She clutched a black box with the gloss of leather, ideal for an engagement ring. Gold string bound it in a double-knotted bow. She reached out her skeletal hand. "I brought Murray a housewarming gift."

Grandma Anna stared at the offering, as if leery of its contents. She smiled and accepted it.

"It's viewed best in the moonlight."

"Thank you, Eveleth. That sounds quite—astronomical. Murray, what do you say?"

The word felt like peanut butter in Murray's mouth. "Thank you."

Grandma Anna handed the box to him. He eyed it momentarily, noting its frigidity, as if it had just been removed from a freezer. What the heck was it? An ice cube? Liquid nitrogen? It couldn't be anything welcoming.

Mrs. Vitikin brushed her hands on her dress, as if the box had been grimy. "So…is Marilyn still stopping by today?"

Grandma Anna wrung the towel with clenched teeth. Her lip trembled. "*Eva.*"

"Oh, I'm sorry, dear. It's been quite some time since I've seen either of them in town."

"You know Eva lives three hours away, Eveleth."

"She does own a car. I wouldn't think an annual trip is asking too much."

Grandma Anna bit her lip to ease the quiver and wet the way for her tongue to lash. "You can leave now, thank you. I'd like to get my gardening done before the humidity rises."

"Of course. I've worn out my welcome as it is."

Mrs. Vitikin turned and hobbled back the way she had come, which struck Murray as odd, seeing how her house was in the opposite direction. He guessed she intended to circle the perimeter, probably prowling for more gossip. He sighed, relieved she had left the premises. His first impression remained unchanged; the woman seemed as creepy and as cold as a bat cave.

Grandma Anna rolled her eyes. "Unbelievable. Why she gave your gift to me is a mystery. Sometimes she is so removed. Yet I suppose it's the thought that counts. She should think more often. Maybe that tongue of hers would stop slipping."

Murray nodded and followed Grandma Anna as she crossed to the garden. She knelt and picked up the gushing hose, regarding the puddle stretched along the mulch. She looked to Murray, who simply shrugged. They both knew the Mrs. Vitikin distraction nearly flooded the flowers. Murray foresaw the end result in Havlock-esque vengeance, like Grandma Anna chopping down her yews. He just hoped Grandma Anna turned off the spigot.

She stood and placed her index finger over the nozzle of the hose. A gentle rain fell on the blooming beauties. She proceeded to circle the garden, showering it like a passing cloud.

Murray's mind wandered out of boredom. He removed the housewarming gift from his pocket. Still cold, the black box dripped condensation from the heat. He turned it over in his hands. While the gold string resembled twine, its texture felt more like a braided strand of hair. Again, he pondered the contents. If Mrs. Vitikin was younger and tech-savvy, he expected a wireless spy camera. Realistically, though, it probably contained something more creepy and peculiar. Maybe a human eyeball or—another box! Like those babushka dolls, a box within a box within a box, the possibilities endless. He needed a distraction. Unknowns drove him crazy.

It's viewed best in the moonlight.

A chill coursed through Murray's veins. Mrs. Vitikin's comment made him think of werewolves. Maybe the box held a silver bullet, and the old hag was a lycanthrope by night, a self-defensive hint of sorts. No, too meaningful. He shook his head, wishing his overactive thoughts would fade. Either way, he would find out the contents come evening. He presumed Lady Luck would see the moon shining brightly.

The remainder of the morning breezed by while the sun peeked suspiciously between the clouds. Grandma Anna fried grilled cheese sandwiches for lunch as Murray looked out the bay window.

He dwelled on Mrs. Vitikin's visit. "Grandma, what happened the last time Pontius got loose?"

Grandma Anna sighed. "I was wondering when you'd ask about that." She flipped the sandwiches with a spatula and turned to face Murray. "Let's see… I think it was sometime in early spring. Cab had just gotten home from church. Mr. Havlock was standing over there by the street, with Pontius at his side. Pontius started barking like crazy. Cab flipped them both the bird and headed up the steps to his porch." She shook her head as she returned to the sizzling griddle. "That was when Havlock dropped the leash and smacked Pontius in the back of the head. He took off across the street like a bat out of Hell. He had his jaws around Cab's leg before he could get in the house. Cab's only defense was the front door, which he slammed on Pontius's head. The stupid mutt took off whining back to his master. Since then, Blossom Boulevard's been a regular soap opera."

Murray's stomach growled. The grilled cheese sandwiches smelled terrific. "What about Cab? Did he get hurt?"

"Ask him sometime. I'm sure he'll be more than happy to show you his battle scars."

The doorbell chimed as if on cue, postponing their conversation for the time being. Grandma Anna turned off the stove and strode out of the kitchen. Her apron flapped all the way to the foyer. Murray looked at the clock on the wall. A quarter past noon. He hoped Aunt Eva had arrived and not another nosy neighbor.

The front door shut, and Murray heard the sound of heels clicking on the hardwood floor.

Aunt Eva entered the kitchen, a vision of comfort in her T-shirt and jeans. "How are you, Murray?"

He stood. "I'm okay."

"Good." Aunt Eva set down her black handbag and hugged Murray. Her perfume made his head swim. Her purple blouse smelled like lilacs. "That's good to hear."

With the embrace and pungency of flowers, a feeling of longing tugged at Murray's heart. He found himself in the midst of Roses in Rushford, his mom arranging a display of white begonias while Aunt Eva busied herself behind the counter. Everything back to normal again. Life was roses.

"Well," Grandma Anna said as she stepped through the doorway.

Murray snapped back to reality as Aunt Eva released him.

"I should probably finish making lunch."

Murray sat back down at the table while Grandma Anna fired up the burners.

Aunt Eva took a seat to his left. "Murray, I came out here today because my apology over the phone wasn't good enough. We both lost someone close to us. I just got so overwhelmed with everything—the funeral, the shop—I'm truly sorry for forgetting about you, and I understand if you won't forgive me." She reached down into her handbag. "Your mother wanted you to have this. I only know because it has your name on it." She set the present on the table; narrow and flat, it was wrapped in plain blue paper with a white gift tag on top.

Murray opened the tag and saw his name scrawled in his mother's handwriting. "What is it?"

Aunt Eva shrugged with a smile. "I have no idea. I found it wrapped like that on her dresser."

Murray picked it up and eyed it. Narrowly shaped, maybe it held a bracelet. First, Mrs. Vitikin's ring box, and now this. He gently peeled off the wrapping. If this had been the last thing his mom touched, he refused to tear it to shreds. As the paper fell to the table, his brow furrowed. A red velvet necklace case. But why would a boy want jewelry?

Aunt Eva leaned in as Grandma Anna stepped away from the stove. "Go ahead. Open it."

Murray did so. To his surprise, the case contained a sleek, black paintbrush with a ruby at the tip of the wood handle.

At some point, Grandma Anna wandered away from the stove. She loomed over Murray. "That's your mother's dagger brush. I bought it for her on her thirteenth birthday."

Murray looked up. "My mom used to paint, too?"

"She tried, but never really took to it."

Murray felt the bristles, long, angled, and rough to the touch. He flinched, and a bead of blood formed on his index finger. "It's sharp."

"Indeed. Most watercolor brushes are composed of sable, but this particular one I came across while vacationing in Venice. The bristles are made of porcupine quills and human hair. It's more for decoration than actual painting, which is probably why it's still so clean."

Murray frowned. "So it doesn't work?"

"You'd have to try it out for yourself, I guess."

Murray nodded, shut the case, and pocketed it. "Thank you, Aunt Eva."

Aunt Eva sifted in her handbag again. "You're welcome, darling. Mother, I brought you something, too. The police returned Marilyn's journal." She set a black leather-bound book on the table. "I thought you might know a good place for safekeeping."

Grandma Anna accepted the memento. "Oh, Eva. Thank you. I know just where to keep it."

"Grandma? I think the grilled cheese might be done."

Grandma Anna whirled and removed the smoking griddle from the burner. She shut off the stove and sighed. "They're done alright. Well done."

Aunt Eva chuckled. "I forgot how much I missed home cooking."

"I beg your pardon?"

"Oh, Mother." Aunt Eva fished around in her bag, continuing to play Santa Claus. "I do have one more thing of Marilyn's."

Grandma Anna smirked. "I bet it's Paul Bunyan this time."

Aunt Eva revealed a crystal vase. It sparkled in the bright sunlight as she set it in the center of the table. "This is for the both of you. I figured you could put that big old rose garden to use."

Grandma Anna's eyes welled with tears. "What do you say, Murray?"

Murray nodded, smiling. "Let's go pick some roses."

"Let's. Eva, are you game? Lunch can wait. Even when it's cold, it's still grilled cheese."

Aunt Eva zipped her handbag. "I'm game."

Later that afternoon, Grandma Anna and Murray said their goodbyes to Aunt Eva. Her heartwarming visit set Murray's mind at ease. While nice to possess a memento to remember his mom by, the journal made his curiosity burn. He pondered her last written words, what she stated about her killer—the pages of which had probably been removed by the police—and how many happy memories she shared. Maybe one day Grandma Anna would let him in on the secrets.

Dinner was served around six—goulash and corn on the cob—and they called it a day by eight o'clock. As Murray shut his bedroom door, he wondered if tomorrow would be as eventful. He hoped to at least stray from the neighborhood and see downtown Windom. He yearned to walk on the shores of Superior and toss rocks into the waves, the things he had done with his mom on vacations.

He pulled off his T-shirt and tossed it by the desk. He was about to slip off his shorts when his hand grazed the bulging right pocket.

The black box.

Murray removed Mrs. Vitikin's glossy gift. He snapped off the gold string and cast it aside. He popped the top and stared blankly at the contents. What could it be? It looked like a dead cockroach. It was about the size of a half-dollar and black with a line of red dots down its back; hairy spikes protruded from its abdomen, nearly disguising its pincer-like feet. Three red feelers poked from the head.

Murray grimaced, on the verge of dropping the box, when Mrs. Vitikin's words came back to him.

It's viewed best in the moonlight.

Murray walked over to the window and set the box on the sill. He opened the double pane. A crescent moon beamed in the dusky sky. Murray took a deep breath of the cool breeze, then picked up the box and held it out the window.

A long hiss cut the air. The black roach started to wriggle around. A second later, it exploded, popping like a firecracker. The box ignited, and flames engulfed Murray's hand. He dropped it outside the window and whirled inside. He shoved his arm under the comforter and pounded on it with his other hand. He stood there for a moment, panting, reluctant to look at the damage. Oddly, he didn't feel an ounce of pain.

His brain fed off the adrenaline. *I looked like Firestorm there for a second. That was pretty cool. But what the heck was that? Missus Vitikin tried to kill me! Boy, Grandma Anna might do the same if I ruined the bed. How am I going to explain this? I don't want to even look. My hand's probably bleeding all over the place. Well, here goes nothing.*

Murray shut his eyes and slowly inched his arm out from under the covers. He snuck a peek and went wide-eyed. Unscathed, he flexed his hand, amazed at the lack of pain. Not even a singe on his fingers. He peeled back the comforter; the underside and sheets were black and smelled burnt.

Without another thought, he slammed the window and dashed to the four-poster. He scrambled beneath the comforter, not about to get caught red-handed. He knew Grandma Anna saw the fireball from one of the windows. If not her, certainly one of the nosy neighbors.

Last-second excuses flitted through Murray's head. No way would Grandma Anna buy the truth. She would never believe Mrs. Vitikin tried to kill him. No choice but to play it safe and lie his tail off.

A knock at the bedroom door.

Grandma Anna poked her head in. Her hair down, she looked dog-tired as she scanned the room. "What's all the raucous about?"

Murray pulled the comforter up to his chin. "I had my window open. It just shut by itself."

"Ah, I see. I thought you might've fallen out of bed." Grandma Anna narrowed her eyes and sniffed the air. "Cab must be burning leaves again. Do you always sleep with the lights on?"

"Sometimes."

"Well, I think it's time to change your habits. Electricity isn't cheap nowadays." Grandma Anna switched off the lights. "See you in the morning."

The door shut, and Murray sighed. He cursed Mrs. Vitikin. Clearly, she despised kids. He definitely would be keeping his distance and watching his back.

His gaze locked on the crescent moon beyond the window, the flaming box etched in his mind. How many nosy neighbors watched it fall? And what was Mrs. Vitikin's intention? Why would she be trying to harm him? Or a better question: how could fire fail to burn him? Was he a mutant like the superheroes in his comics? How cool would that be?

The more questions that plagued Murray, the heavier his eyelids became. He soon nodded off and embraced the prowling nightmares.

Chapter 4

The next morning, perfume roused Murray from his slumber. He blinked away the cobwebs. Grandma Anna crouched at the bedside with a warm smile on her face.

She rustled Murray's tousled hair. "Rise and shine, dandelion. I thought I'd wake you up a bit earlier today since I have to leave for work at nine."

"Work?" Murray replied groggily as he pushed himself up on his elbows.

"Yes, work. The nursing home, remember? Thankfully, it's my short week. I work today and Friday, then the rest of the week is ours." Grandma Anna stood, walked to the end of the room, and opened the window. "Let's see how long it stays open this time."

The exploding roach stoked Murray's memory. After last night, he knew Lady Luck had left the building. The Macabe Place was probably a good eighty years old; the window wouldn't budge in a hurricane.

"So," Grandma Anna continued, "I forgot to ask. What was in that box Missus Vitikin gave you?"

The truth prodded Murray's conscience. What was it,

indeed? A cockroach? An exploding cockroach? "Nothing. It was empty."

"Empty? I'm really beginning to wonder if that woman's in her right mind. She met me at the doorstep this morning with my newspaper and a pile of ashes in hand. She told me Missus Muldoon saw the house breathe fire last night."

Murray chuckled nervously. "Breathe fire?"

"Imagine that."

"Sounds pretty crazy."

"Well, that's why I call her Crazy Daisy. Although Missus Vitikin did say she passed a patch of burnt grass on her way over here. So who knows? Maybe that wasn't a bonfire I smelled last night. *Maybe* Havlock's up to his old tricks again."

"Why? Because of me?"

"I don't think he ever has a reason. He's as curmudgeon as they come. You'd better believe I'll check the lawn on my way out." Grandma Anna paused in the doorway. "Why don't you get dressed? I'll have breakfast ready when you come down."

"Okay."

Grandma Anna shut the door behind her. Guilt prodded Murray's conscience. Maybe he should tell the truth. On second thought, Grandma Anna might think he was *stretching* the truth. Or maybe she'd think the week's stress had finally gotten to him. A crazy admission could earn him a seat in a shrink's office.

He crawled out of bed. He stared at the burnt bedding. He needed to do something with it. But what? He quickly folded up the comforter and shoved it under his bed. He balled up the sheet and stashed it in a dresser drawer. Seeing how it was summer, he would tell Grandma Anna the warm nights made him restless. It seemed plausible. Satisfied, Murray dug out a pair of blue sweat shorts and a white tank top. Soon after, he headed downstairs en route to the kitchen.

Grandma Anna smiled as he sat down at the table. "Good morning. Of course, it would be a great morning if I didn't have to work. I would much rather spend the day with you. It's too bad two nurses are on vacation."

"When will you be back?"

"Five o'clock. We'll have the evening all to ourselves."

"So, I'll be home alone today?"

"Of course not, sweetie." Grandma Anna set a bowl of oatmeal and a spoon on Murray's placemat. "I called Cab last night. He said he'd love to have you over."

"But I don't even know him."

"And I do. He's lived on this block as long as I have. He even has a couple of grandkids about your age."

Murray looked out the bay window expecting to see Cab enjoying his morning juice, but the porch was vacant and the shades drawn.

"Everyone needs a friend, Murray, and Cab's as good as they come."

"I just wish there was someone my age."

"A friend is a friend." Grandma Anna sat down at the table and took a long sip of her tea. "Don't worry. I wouldn't leave you with someone I didn't trust. Especially not after all you've been through. You have my word."

Murray stared down at his oatmeal and nodded. Still, the thought of hanging out with an old man gave him the willies. Sure, Cab seemed nice the day he met him, but he probably harbored a dark side, like his mom's killer. How could he possibly trust another man in his life?

He's lived on this block as long as I have.

Grandma Anna's comment sparked Murray's thinking cap. He wondered if his mom knew Cab when she was younger. And if so, had she trusted him? Since the tragedy, Murray questioned every one of her past decisions.

He gazed across the boulevard at Cab's house. White

and two stories tall, the latticed porch complimented the co-balt blue shutters. A weather vane spun in the wind on the westernmost gable. Overgrown elders with white flowers and purplish-black berries shaded the short green lawn.

"So," Grandma Anna said, breaking a long silence, "in an hour or so I'll walk you over there."

Murray looked out the window, trying to distract his worry. "Can we at least go to the lake today?"

"I don't see why not. If you'd like, we could have a picnic by the shore and watch the sun set."

Murray turned and faced Grandma Anna. "Can we? That'd be cool."

"Consider it a date. We'll go straight after work. We'll dine on jelly sandwiches and Cheetos."

Murray grinned. "Do you think I'll have a little time to paint after breakfast?"

"If you hurry up and eat that oatmeal."

Murray dove in with a heaping spoonful. While the lake would provide a much-needed distraction, painting would take his mind off things, such as spending the day with a stranger. After all, there had to be more to Windom than grumpy old neighbors.

Murray yearned for a shore where he could anchor his drifting ship.

Murray entered the attic and noticed Grandma Anna had lit the candelabra beforehand. For what reason, who knew? He figured it set the mood, creating a relaxing atmosphere to paint. A black mass filled his periphery and his gaze locked on the dark room. Again, he pondered the secrecy. What was Grandma Anna hiding? And couldn't she just use her bedroom if she wanted privacy?

Murray shook off the prying thoughts and peeled his eyes from the curtain. He looked to the corner window and walked over to the easel. Grandma Anna did him a favor by providing a blank canvas and fresh watercolors. She even pulled out the stool and adorned it with a green cushion. A blue drop cloth protected the floor. The urge to paint prodded Murray.

He sat down and stared at the emptiness. His emotions brewed in his subconscious, but he pushed them back, striving to bring good thoughts to the forefront. While his mood brightened, he worried about getting babysat. The last time he painted a storm raged inside him—anger, sorrow, resentment. Today, he wanted to create something happier, more calming. His mom smiled in his mind's eye.

He picked up a filbert brush and dipped it into the red. Yet instead of blood, he began painting his mom's favorite dress. With that, matching shoes. He mixed the red and white to make pink, coloring in her face. After a bit, he finished the portrait, save for her beautiful flowing hair. Yellow cascaded down her shoulders, stirring in the breeze.

Murray set down the brush and eyed his artwork. He couldn't wait to show Grandma Anna. He knew she would fall in love with it. Maybe he could even hang this one on the wall rather than in the dark room. His brow furrowed. Still, something was missing. It needed a dash of realism. He remembered Aunt Eva's gift. He withdrew the case from his pocket and opened it on the tray. While it was supposedly for decorative purposes only, the rough bristles would add the perfect texture to the hair.

He scraped the brush against the canvas, amazed as he painted strands, waves, and curls. He was so caught up in the strokes he forgot the roughness of the bristles. The dagger brush slashed through his mom's hairline and across her face.

Murray sat there for a moment, staring at the damage in

disbelief. He destroyed his entire creation with one swipe. The suppressed anger bubbled over like a volcano. Everything was ruined. There was no touching up torn canvas. And there would be no showing it off to Grandma Anna.

Murray whipped the brush across the room and shoved the easel. It toppled over and collided with the nearby candelabra, the candle falling on top of it. The unpainted canvas and wooden frame caught fire. Murray's heart leaped to his throat.

"Aw, heck!"

His brain flashed back to the debacle in his bedroom. He needed to snuff the flames before he burned down the whole house. He yanked up the drop cloth, knocking over the stool. As he was about to throw it down, he was mesmerized for a split second. He watched the candle wax spread across the canvas as his mom's face began to char. He thought about his last encounter with fire and how his hand emerged unscathed. With the sheet in his left hand, he crouched and stretched out his right, reaching into the flames. His hand trembled, worried that it was going to hurt. Instead, it merely tickled.

Murray snapped back to reality and tossed down the drop cloth. He stomped on the flames in a frenzy. To his relief, they extinguished with ease.

"What in the blazes is going on up here?"

Murray whirled, startled by Grandma Anna's voice from the top of the spiral. She marched across the attic.

Murray's brain rummaged through excuses. "Sorry, Grandma! I accidentally knocked over the easel and hit the candle and started a fire. I used the sheet to put it out. I'm really sorry."

Grandma Anna's glare turned to concern. "I knew I shouldn't have had the candelabra so close. Are you okay, sweetie? Are you hurt?"

He looked at his hand. Unharmed, not burnt in the slightest. "No. I'm fine. I just…got scared for a second."

Grandma Anna blew out the remaining candles. "Why don't you pick up the stool and I'll clean up the rest?" Murray obeyed, relieved that he dodged a bullet. "Well, the easel's okay, but whatever you painted is done for. Unless you want it to be abstract."

"I'm not so sure painting's for me."

"Nonsense. Accidents happen. You can try again another day. Now go wash up."

Murray left Grandma Anna with the mess and headed for the spiral. He spotted the dagger brush lying near the dark room. It could stay there. It ruined enough for one day.

⊛ ⊛ ⊛

The dreaded hour arrived.

Grandma Anna asked Murray once more if he wanted her to accompany him, but he shook his head. So she shrugged and left for work.

Soon after, Murray exited the house and headed down the driveway. The morning felt mild, even with the overcast sky. Murray hoped the forecast remained stable. The picnic would definitely set his mind at ease.

He sighed. He was as nervous as a goody-goody called to the principal's office. He could not stop thinking about the last man who tried to buy his friendship. He fought off flashbacks of his mom's killer in the cheap leisure suit and sunglasses handing him a mint condition, Number One issue of *Dr. Doom*. The man had bought his trust. Murray refused to let it happen again. At the same time, he made a mental note that Grandma Anna considered Cab a good friend. He took her word for it.

He crossed the deserted boulevard and ascended the concrete drive. His eyes locked on the bronze four-door Cadillac. A shiver racked his spine. While different in color and lacking tinted windows, it was the same model as the murderer's. And yesterday, Cab suited up as well, even offered Murray lemonade, an effort to buy his trust. The similarities were uncanny. Maybe Cab was a wolf in sheep's clothing.

"Well, good mornin', Murray!"

Murray looked up and saw Cab stepping onto the porch. Dressed in brown slacks and a blue, button-down twill shirt, his head shined as if recently moisturized, glistening like the tumbler in his hand. The screen door slammed behind him.

Murray cleared his throat, fending off the butterflies in his stomach. "Good morning. My grandma said she'd be home around five."

"Lovely! That'll give us plenty of time to get acquainted. Care for an orange juice or…a lemonade?"

Alarm bells sounded in Murray's head. The bait to lure his trust. He bit his lip. "No, thanks. I just had breakfast."

"Suit yourself. Have a seat. Make yourself at home."

Cab gestured to a matching pair of white wicker chairs. Murray sat down while Cab leaned against the porch railing, sipping his orange juice.

"So, Murray, what do you think of Windom?"

Murray shifted in his seat, struggling to still his bouncing leg as he stared at the floorboards. "It seems okay, I guess. I haven't been off this street yet."

"You're pullin' my leg, son. You haven't been downtown?"

"Uh-uh."

"You haven't been to the lake?"

"Hopefully tonight. Grandma said we'd have a picnic there when she got home."

Cab drained his tumbler and set it on the porch railing.

"Now that sounds like a plan. There's nothin' more breath-takin' than Superior. It's like lookin' out at the ocean, only seein' the ships and the water. Come wintertime, I see those UMD students surfin' at high tide. I gather they get the same feelin'."

Murray nodded, wishing more than ever that he sat on the rocky shore rather than an old man's porch. He looked up and met Cab's gaze.

Cab pointed his thumb over his shoulder. "So, how's things goin' with you two so far?"

Murray shrugged. "Okay."

"She's a good woman, Murray. She reminds me of my wife, Georgia, God bless her soul. She's been an angel to me since I moved here. And that's somethin' you don't see on this block."

"What do you mean?"

"You've met the neighbors, son. You tell me."

"I've only met Missus Vitikin and Mister Havlock."

"And they made a good impression on you, right?"

Murray's gaze trained on Mrs. Vitikin's house. The huge, dark green yew trees gave him the willies. He knew they were poisonous from the days in his mom's flower shop, quite uncommon to have growing in a front yard. They certainly proved to be an omen thus far.

Cab half-smiled. "I take that as a 'no'."

Murray shook his head.

"Yeah, Eveleth has that kind of effect on you. She's got more than a few screws loose."

"You mean she's crazy, right?"

"Hey, you said it, not me. I would've thought you saw her in the bay window by now."

Murray's eyes darted to the house across the way. He glimpsed the old hag as she sidestepped behind the curtain. He looked to Cab, overcome with unease.

Cab grinned and picked up his tumbler. "I need a refill. Want to take me up on that lemonade yet?"

"No, thanks."

The screen door slammed. Murray looked back to Mrs. Vitikin's bay window. She stood in plain view with a lighter in hand. She raised a candle and lit it. A crooked grin cracked her haggard face.

Murray broke out in a cold sweat. Had Mrs. Vitikin spied on him as he knocked over the easel? Of course, she had; she tried setting him on fire once already.

Squealing tires made Murray jump. He looked up the block. A weathered gray Cruiser roared around the corner. He glanced back to Mrs. Vitikin's window. She was gone, the curtains swaying in her wake.

Cab stepped outside with a full tumbler in hand. He sat down beside Murray. "There goes the neighborhood."

Mr. Havlock scowled as he passed by and whipped the Cruiser up his driveway. It jolted to a stop a foot from the garage door. Mr. Havlock climbed out, slammed the driver's side door, and stormed into the house.

Murray looked to Cab. "What's his problem anyways?"

"Beats me. You want to ask him, be my guest."

"Heck, if *Cujo* wasn't waiting for me."

Cab chuckled, his deep voice reverberating in the tumbler when he brought it to his lips. "You can say that again. I'm guessin' you found out he's not kid-friendly."

"Yeah. Yesterday. I thought he was gonna have me for lunch."

"Well, don't worry none. He's far from Cab-friendly, too."

"What do you mean?" Murray played stupid, eager to hear the story firsthand.

Cab raised his fine brow. "Don't tell me you don't know? It's the talk of the block."

"I heard Missus Vitikin say that Pontius got loose once."

"Let loose is more like it. The codger was waitin' for me to come home. I get out of my car, and he starts rantin'. He says a black man's got no business livin' in a white house. Now I'm a peaceful man, Murray. I just flip him the bird and head for my porch. Sure, I hear Pontius barkin' up a storm, but I don't realize the mutt's at my heels 'til I'm on my steps. He got a hold of my leg and would've gnawed it off if I hadn't slammed his head in the screen door. Ever since then, Havlock and that hellhound have kept their distance."

"Didn't you call the cops?"

"Seein' how they're a good ten miles from here, I called it even. We both got our battle scars." Cab leaned forward and set his glass on the railing. "Besides which, the police tend to make me out as the bad guy."

"So, there's no cops in this town?"

"None whatsoever. That's why we all do our best to get along."

"That's crazy. Back in Rushford, the sheriff seemed to know everybody."

"Well, like I said, when you're the only black man around, you stick out like a deer in a lion's den."

Murray considered asking about downtown Windom when a glint caught his eye. An old woman with bright orange hair and a pair of long shears shambled toward the garden. Face etched in a permanent frown, her canary yellow sundress camouflaged her amidst the six-foot sunflowers and tulips.

Cab checked his Rolex. "Nine o'clock on the dot."

"Missus Muldoon?"

"The one and only."

"Does she always look that angry?"

"Son, that's her happy face. She's another one to steer clear of. Between her and Havlock, I don't know who hates kids more. Last call for lemonade." Murray shook his head. Cab grabbed his empty glass. "Alrighty. I'll be back in a flash then."

The moment Cab entered the house, Murray felt he was being watched. He glanced at Mrs. Vitikin's house. There she stood in the bay window. She blew out the candle.

Murray looked back to Mrs. Muldoon. His jaw dropped. Mrs. Muldoon made a chopping motion with her shears while exchanging glares with Mrs. Vitikin. She stopped at the foot of the garden. She opened her shears. Murray gaped as she reached to decapitate a blooming sunflower, the tallest of the bunch, and above all, the symbol of happiness.

Mrs. Muldoon whirled and leered at Murray, her frown twisting into a scowl. The shears snapped shut before her face.

Murray glanced over to Mrs. Vitikin's house. The curtains closed.

Murray looked back to Mrs. Muldoon. She slowly approached with the shears by her side.

The screen door slammed. Murray leaped out of his chair, his heart hurtling into his throat.

"Whoa there! It's just the door. Damn thing sounds like a shotgun, but trust me, everyone around here's too old to be playin' the Hatfields and McCoys."

Murray stared, speechless.

Cab followed his line of sight, and upon understanding, he narrowed his gaze. "Have a seat, son, and let me do the talkin'."

"Mister Linlith."

"Well, good mornin', Daisy. How goes the gardenin'?"

"Hot. I'm burning up as usual."

"That's a redhead for you. Always simmerin'. Always breathin' fire."

"Meaning?"

"Meanin' Murray and I are off to the air conditionin'. Happy prunin', Daisy. C'mon, son."

Cab turned his back on Mrs. Muldoon and led Murray inside the house. Murray heard Mrs. Muldoon's shears snap shut seconds before the door slammed behind them.

Murray was glad Cab kept an eye on him. Had he been home alone, Mrs. Muldoon might have taken advantage of the situation, whatever the motive. He knew one thing: he didn't trust an ornery old woman with garden tools.

Murray lingered in the entryway—immediately noticing the refreshing cool air—and eyed his new surroundings. The large den donned off-white carpet, a beige leather sofa, and a matching recliner. A glass coffee table served as a center-piece, cluttered with a well-read bible and the contents of a *Star Tribune*. A handful of family photographs adorned the caramel walls amidst a scattering of wood crosses. Beyond, an eat-in kitchen and three windows overlooked the backyard.

Cab sighed, shaking his head. "Crazy Daisy." He gestured toward the sofa. "Make yourself comfy, son." Murray did so while Cab sat in the recliner. "I'm not usually that un-friendly, but baldies and redheads get along like bakin' soda and vinegar, if you know what I mean."

"So, why do you call her Crazy Daisy?"

"Well, ever since last year I've been noticin' some things. They never had a suspect for the fire, you know."

Murray's brows arched, his interest peaked. "Fire?"

"The Fennely Farm. About a block from here. What's left of it anyhow. The house and the barn burnt down."

"What happened?"

"Fire department said it was electrical. But I did some nosin' around myself one day, once the dust had settled. You see, Frank Fennely was a good Christian, sat in the front pew every Sunday. One time he got to thumpin' his bible around Daisy, she went off like a hydrant, spoutin' all sorts of curses and hell and damnation. I heard it all from my porch, had to intervene and get Frank on his way. But I'll never forget her last words to him." Cab paused, letting the storm cloud hang in the air. "'I'll see you burn in a pit of snakes and brimstone.'"

Murray's jaw slacked. "She said that?"

"God's truth. I never gave her comment much thought at the time, 'til Frank and his family went up in flames."

"So how do you think the fire started?"

"I don't think. I know, son. All that's left of the farm is the silo, being made of brick and all. The house and the barn were straight-up cedar. When I went snoopin', I found the culprit, like a cannon full of gunpowder. A whole nest of scorchroaches."

"Scorchroaches?"

Cab leaned forward and looked over his spectacles. "That's right. Native round these parts. They look like cockroaches, but if you shine a light on 'em, they explode. Nature's time bombs. And they don't leave a trace of evidence at a crime scene, if you catch my drift."

The other night flashed before Murray's eyes. The box. The insect. The moonlight. His hand engulfed in flames.

Grandma Anna's voice rang in Murray's head: *Missus Muldoon saw the house breathe fire last night.*

Murray felt numb. Mrs. Vitikin gave him a scorchroach! Now he understood what she meant by a housewarming gift. She probably intended to torch Grandma Anna's house like the Fennely Farm. While Cab pointed the finger at Mrs. Muldoon, Murray wondered if it wasn't her neighbor.

"You really think Missus Muldoon set the farm on fire?"

Cab removed his glasses, set them on the coffee table, and rubbed his eyes. "Like I said, I don't think, I know. I saw her come out of that silo one day. The strange thing is, though, there's no way that's the breedin' grounds. She's gettin' 'em from somewhere else, somewhere dark and damp. Maybe Eveleth's basement, since Daisy doesn't have one."

Murray considered whether to tell Cab about the house-warming gift. "I think you're right. Missus Vitikin gave me a scorchroach yesterday." Cab raised his brows, taken aback. "She gave me a box. I opened it last night, and it had a black bug in it. She told me to put it in the moonlight. Well, I did… and the whole thing blew up in my hand."

Cab furrowed his brow. "That sounds like a scorchroach alright. You've only been here two days, and she tried to hurt you? I've been here a good twenty years just expectin' to find one in my mailbox."

"But why? I didn't do anything to her."

"Evil Eveleth," Cab replied, as if that answered Murray's question. "And Crazy Daisy. Hmm." He ran his hands over his head as if he still had hair. "I think it's finally comin', son."

"What? What's coming?"

"The Last Days. If they're after you, they'll be comin' at your grandmother next. They've already been watchin' your house like a hawk."

Murray glanced up, paranoid Mrs. Muldoon lurked in the window behind closed curtains. "I still don't get it. Why would they team up to hurt us? And Grandma Anna's lived here for years. Wouldn't they have already done something by now?"

Cab leaned back in the recliner. "I hate to break this to you, son, but *you're* the reason why. I can't explain it quite yet; I just know you're the only kid in town. And every time one shows up, they disappear like mornin' dew, with some made-up story to cover the tracks."

Murray felt more paranoid than ever. How could he go back to Grandma Anna's house knowing her neighbors were out to get them? How could he sleep at night? He was glad he sat with Cab right now. In fact, Murray needed to ensure Cab watched him when Grandma Anna went to work.

He looked to the old man for reassurance. "So what do I do? What if Missus Vitikin tries something else?"

Cab steepled his fingers in thought. "Well, if she gives you anythin' strange again, anythin' at all, bring it to me. Besides that, keep your distance. I know she lives next door and all, but I wouldn't let her in the house."

"But Grandma Anna will."

"I know that, son. She doesn't know any better. She's too nice of a person. I see her bringin' herbs to Eveleth all the time. It makes me wonder what she's up to."

They sat in silence for a moment. Murray's head spun. The more he thought about Mrs. Vitikin and Mrs. Muldoon, the more he felt like a character in *The Twilight Zone*. He couldn't very well tell Grandma Anna to ignore her neighbors or not let them in the house. She would think him crazy. Plus, she wasn't about to listen to a kid who suffered emotional distress after losing his mom and all. He would need to watch his back and keep his guard up.

Cab stood and stretched with a groan. "You know what we need to do? Get some fresh air." He reached into his pocket and withdrew a set of keys. "Let's go for a ride. Neither of those crazy ladies drive."

Murray stood, eyes locked on the keys "Where are we going?"

"The brambles. I've got somethin' there you're gonna need."

✪ ✪ ✪

After locking the front door, Cab and Murray headed down the porch steps. A loud *crack* snatched Murray's attention. He looked across the boulevard. Mrs. Vitikin stood on her front steps shaking a black rug. Her gray dress billowed in the breeze. Cab unlocked the Cadillac's passenger side door, and Murray climbed in. He raised his brow at the blue-green interior.

Cab turned the ignition, and the engine roared like an old tiger. "The nerve of that woman. Pretendin' like all she's doin' is shakin' out dust. This is the worst I've seen it, Murray, and I know it's just because you're over here. They don't want people makin' friends…and takin' sides."

As the Cadillac backed onto the boulevard, Murray spotted a wisp of orange amidst the sunflowers. There Mrs. Muldoon stood, leering at them from the middle of her garden.

Murray shook his head as they turned the corner and traveled up Philodendron Drive. "Wow. I can't believe I moved to Crazy Town."

Cab glanced over at him. "You know, son, I never did tell you how sorry I was about your mother. She was a real sweetheart. A real good woman."

"Thanks."

Murray gazed out the windshield, fighting off the painful reminder of his loss. A flashback of the black Cadillac haunted him. So this was what it looked like from a murderer's point of view. If only his mom hadn't been there to see it.

Cab rolled down his window. "Believe it or not, Windom's not as crazy as it seems. You just ended up on the wrong block. Wait 'til you're at the lake later. You'll see what I mean."

Murray nodded, praying he was right. The Cadillac slowed to a turtle's pace as it approached the intersection of Rosebud Road and Philodendron Drive.

Cab pointed across Murray's lap. "That's the Fennely Farm, that big ol' eyesore there."

Murray followed Cab's finger. On the north side of Rosebud Road sat the blackened remnants spanning the length of the block. A rotted worm fence encircled the perimeter.

In the distance, dead cedars drooped over a charred foundation. To the left, an unscathed silo made of crumbling red brick. Beyond rustled an acre of weeds and crabgrass, possibly once a cornfield.

Murray couldn't break his stare off the silo, thinking about the scorchroaches. "It's kind of creepy."

Cab grinned. "And haunted by cows."

They shared a chuckle as the houses gradually dwindled away. Murray expected to see downtown, but instead woodland surrounded them.

Cab squinted as they approached a street sign marked Sequin Street. "I usually park just around the corner."

The Cadillac turned left at the intersection and parked beside the tree line.

Murray's stomach knotted. What if a maniac lurked in the woods? Or what if Cab was a madman waiting to get him alone? Maybe he worked for Mrs. Vitikin and Mrs. Muldoon, and he planned to make Murray disappear.

Murray needed to act fast and steer Cab away from the woods.

Cab frowned. "You don't look so hot, son. Don't worry. I bought the lot from the Fennelys some time ago. I used to own the one behind it, too, but I sold it to Missus Crestwick. You wouldn't believe what she's got hidden in there."

Murray sized up Cab. He seemed to be at least seventy years old. Harmless enough, but Murray's unease raged when he thought about the woods.

Cab opened his door. "Trust me, son. Your grandmother wouldn't let a nutcase babysit her only grandson. I'm just a borin' old man who does nothin' but hold up his porch every day. Unless you'd rather sit in the car and hang out 'til Havlock comes by?"

Murray knew Cab was right. He had overreacted and let his fears get the best of him. Sooner or later he would need to confront them, in one way or another. And really, what was so scary about some woods in the daytime?

Cab exited the car, and Murray reluctantly followed suit. Birches swayed for blocks, and the road glittered strangely in the sunlight, as if someone shook out all the sequins of an evening dress.

Cab waved. "C'mon. This way."

They crossed the vacant street to the dense tree line. Murray squinted ahead. The woods cast heavy shadows. Silence lingered, save for the leaves rustling in the breeze.

Murray lagged a good five feet behind Cab as the wavering shadows swallowed them. His eyes darted like a doe's during hunting season. Thoughts of bears and wolves and inconspicuous booby traps badgered his brain. He glanced from tree to tree, brush to brush. And even though the forest shade and wind felt cool, sweat dripped from his forehead. He eyed Cab. The old man got along easily, without the use of a cane, as if he hiked on a weekly basis. Certainly limber enough to strangle a kid in the woods. Everyone Murray had met thus far in town seemed crazy. Who was to say Cab wasn't conspiring with them?

Cab stopped abruptly. Murray did the same, keeping his distance.

Cab pointed ahead. "See those brambles there?" Murray gazed at the plant life beyond. He nodded when he spotted a cluster of huge red shrubs in the distance. "That's my safe. It's thick with prickles. If anyone ever tried trespassin', they'd definitely come out bleedin'."

Murray arched a brow. "What do you mean? You're hiding something in there?"

"Follow the leader. I wouldn't show this to just anybody."

They ventured deeper into the woods until they stood at the base of the brambles. They loomed a good seven feet high. The prickers looked more like thorns; the raspberries on the leaves resembled beads of blood. Overgrown and circular, the bush proved too thick to see through.

Cab grasped a branch protruding near his midsection. "Right here's the door." He gave it a tug and an arched entrance opened inward. "And this is my little hideaway."

Murray entered the enclosure as Cab shut the camouflaged door behind them. A woodshed with slate shingles sat in the center of the brambles. A silver combination lock secured the double doors. Overhead, a pergola of poison ivy. Murray looked up at Cab upon recognizing the white berries, while self-consciously hugging his arms close to his body.

Cab noted Murray's gaze. "That's my security guard." He gestured at the double doors. "And that's my safe."

"The shed?"

"What were you expectin', son? A vault?"

Murray shook his head, speechless. Cab approached the doors and turned the dial on the combination lock. It clicked, and he stepped back and opened the doors. They swung wide as far as the hinges would allow.

Cab placed a hand on Murray's shoulder. "So, see anythin' you like? My grandson would've loved it, but I guess he's not comin' down for a bit. It would've been an early birthday present."

Murray glanced from wall to wall, adjusting his eyes to the shadows. "How old is he?"

"Ten next month. I'll give you a clue. You can ride it, but it's not a lawnmower."

Murray scanned the dusty contents. Pegboard covered each wall, from which dangled rusty trowels, shears, and other various garden tools. On the floor were cardboard boxes, a lawnmower, a handful of metal folding chairs, and a matching card table. Poking out from beneath the table…a fire engine red bicycle.

Murray's eyes widened, along with his smile. "The bike?"

Cab nodded.

"Really? But it's your grandson's. Why don't you just keep it here 'til you see him again?"

Cab thought for a moment as he stared at the shiny bicycle. "I could, but I don't think Keaton will be back anytime soon. My son and I had a fallin' out." He removed his glasses, rubbed his eyes quickly, and cleared his throat. "I just bought it last month. I don't think the dust has quite settled on it."

Murray could barely remember the last time he rode a bike. He owned a Huffy back in Rushford, but everything fell within walking distance. Much the same as Windom, or so he assumed. Still, he wondered if by accepting the gift he wasn't pouring salt on Cab's fresh wounds. Unable to see his son and grandson until who knew when seemed to be a knife in the heart.

"Are you sure it's okay?"

"Positive."

"Wow! Thanks a million!"

"Thank me when it comes in handy. I don't doubt that it will."

✪ ✪ ✪

Murray and Cab left the brambles and the woods a short while later with the bicycle in tow. Cab heaved it into the Cadillac's trunk, and they proceeded to make their way back to Blossom Boulevard.

When they arrived at the intersection of Rosebud Road and Philodendron Drive, Cab brought the Cadillac to a complete stop. "Well, what do you know? Crazy Daisy's at it again."

Murray followed Cab's gaze out the driver's side window. Mrs. Muldoon shuffled across Rosebud Road with her hands stuffed in the pockets of her sundress. Her eyes locked on the thicket before her, where she disappeared into the dense shadows.

Murray looked back to Cab, whose eyes trained on the swaying bushes. "Where's she going?"

"Back home, no doubt. And I'm goin' to catch her red-handed."

"With what?"

"Scorchroaches, son. That's what."

The Cadillac shot across the intersection. Cab pushed fifty miles per hour, his hands white-knuckled on the steering wheel, leaning toward the windshield. Murray double-checked his seat belt and braced himself, his right foot digging into the floor as if he could press the brake. The bald tires screeched around the corner of Blossom Boulevard. Murray clutched the edge of the seat, all the while dreading a rollover. Wide-eyed, Cab glanced frantically as they approached Mrs. Muldoon's yard.

A glint at the edge of the garden snatched Cab and Murray's gaze like a magnet. Mrs. Muldoon's shears jutted from the sunflowers. The Cadillac jolted as it barreled up Cab's driveway and shrieked to a halt.

Cab unbuckled his seat belt and threw open the door. "Stay here. And keep an eye on my car keys."

"But—"

Cab hopped out the door, slamming it behind him. He hurried alongside his house toward the backyard. Daisy vanished into thin air.

Murray shook his head. Cab seemed as crazy as the rest of the neighbors. The old man was hell-bent on catching Mrs. Muldoon with a pocketful of scorchroaches, which were only circumstantial evidence at this point. Heck, she could probably toss them into the sunlight as if they were merely firecrackers and walk away scot-free. And false accusations would surely stir up a civil war.

A hard object jabbed Murray in the shoulder. He jumped and whirled in his seat. Mrs. Vitikin stood beside the car. She pulled her cane back through the passenger's side window.

She bent to eye level, her thick perfume suffocating Murray, oddly smelling of sandalwood. "Where's Mister Linlith?" She rapped her cane against the door. "Well, boy, where is he?"

Murray pointed his thumb over his shoulder. "Next door…with the scorchroaches."

Flames danced in Mrs. Vitikin's narrowed eyes. Her lip curled, baring her discolored teeth. Murray knew he struck a nerve. But maybe he crossed the line. He wondered for a split-second if he should lock the doors and roll up the windows.

Mrs. Vitikin sneered. "So I gather your gift was house-warming enough?" She grabbed Murray's wrist and looked at his hand as he tried to twist free. She sneered and let him go. "Maybe next time you'll be on andirons."

Murray gulped, ensuring control of his voice. "You don't scare me."

"Yet your bottom lip trembles. Be wary, as your mother was. You're a stone's throw from hellfire."

Mrs. Vitikin hobbled off around the corner of Cab's house. Murray bit his lip in an attempt to still it. His right knee bounced uncontrollably. Something about the old woman scared him. Something more than the scorchroaches. And Murray knew his mom experienced the same firsthand. Had she been fireproof, too? He couldn't help but wonder. Racking his brain, he failed to recall any past incidents.

He took a deep breath. He turned in his seat and scanned the adjacent yards. He could not believe what transpired in the last few minutes. Before long, Cab's hands would be full with the neighborhood hags.

Mrs. Muldoon, eyes wild and red as her hair, stomped into her front yard. Her face twisted in anger and surprise. Mrs. Vitikin and Cab appeared at her heels. Murray leaned his ear toward the window and heard their discourse loud and clear.

Mrs. Vitikin stopped, raised her cane, and slammed it into the grass like a pickax. "Daisy!"

Mrs. Muldoon turned and glared at her followers. Cab paused behind Mrs. Vitikin, fists clenched at his side.

Mrs. Vitikin took a step, using her cane as it was intended. "I demand to know what has you so hot and bothered!"

Daisy placed her hands on her hips and pursed her lips to spit fire. "Out of the blue, Mister Linlith is accusing me of arson! Arson!"

Cab lifted his right fist and pointed. "Just empty your pockets, woman! Empty 'em! I saw you leave the Fennely Farm! I know you weren't pickin' poppies!"

"No! Clover!"

Mrs. Muldoon turned out her pockets and handfuls of white clover poured onto the grass. Cab's jaw dropped. Murray did a double take. Mrs. Vitikin and Mrs. Muldoon glared at him as he looked up. Murray wondered if Cab wasn't crazy after all.

Mrs. Muldoon sneered. "Happy, Mister Linlith?"

Cab shook his head, his eyes so wide Murray thought they might explode. "I know what you're up to. And I'll be damned if I let you get away with it."

Mrs. Vitikin nudged Cab's shoe with her cane. "Is that your apology? I think one's in order. Unless picking flowers is a crime."

"Lord knows it is! That's trespassin', not to mention destruction of private property!"

"Then call the police, you crazy old coot. Make a bad situation worse."

"Maybe I will." The women huffed, turned their backs, and walked off toward Mrs. Muldoon's house. "Or maybe I'll handle the situation myself!" Cab rested his chin on his chest for a moment and stared at the pile of clover, the petals scattering across the lawn in the breeze. He kicked the flowers and marched over to the Cadillac. He poked his glistening head through the driver's side window. "I think it's safe, son. How 'bout an early lunch? I know I worked up an appetite."

Murray climbed out of the car and shut the door. "Sounds good to me."

Murray eagerly followed Cab up the porch steps. He glanced over his shoulder. Deserted, the block appeared peaceful beneath its picket fence facade. Murray wondered how his mom survived the madness. She had been strong-willed; the same quality drove her as a child. Murray knew he inherited her best trait. He refused to let Grandma Anna's neighbors drive him crazy.

Murray and Cab lunched on TV trays while they watched the Minnesota Twins trounce the Milwaukee Brewers. Cab cooked ham and Swiss sandwiches and tomato soup. Murray devoured his serving. He guessed the morning events burned some serious calories. Cab offered to fix another sandwich, but Murray politely declined.

After finishing lunch, Cab switched off the TV and brought their trays into the kitchen. He returned with two blue tumblers of cola in hand. Murray grabbed one and followed Cab to the porch. There they sat and sipped in silence, glancing up and down the deserted block, both contemplating the calm before the storm.

Murray eyed Cab's watch. Half past noon. Four and a half hours until the picnic. He felt the afternoon dragging.

Cab took a long draw from his drink. "How about takin' that bike for a spin? Now's the best time for it. The street's empty and everybody's indoors. What do you say?"

Murray's gaze wandered from house to house. He yearned to ride the bike since they walked it out of the brambles. It would be a welcoming change from holding up the porch. Murray leaned forward. The more he entertained the idea, the closer he inched to the edge of his seat. "Can I have the car keys? I'll open the trunk."

Cab set his tumbler on the floor and dug into his right pocket. He tossed Murray the keys. "Sure thing. Let me haul it out, though. That'll be my weightliftin' for the day."

"Alright!"

Murray downed the rest of his cola, set the tumbler down, and dashed to the Cadillac. He quickly unlocked the trunk, and it sprang open. He grinned upon seeing the fire engine red bicycle situated atop the spare tire.

Cab rounded the bumper and reached into the trunk. He lifted the bike out and let it drop with a bounce. He pushed down the kickstand as Murray shut the trunk. "Have at it, son." Cab scanned the boulevard. "The coast is clear. Just do me a favor and stay on the block. I'm guessin' your grandmother wouldn't want you wanderin' off."

"You got it!"

Cab headed back to the porch, whistling and acting like the neighborhood watch. Murray looked the bike over. Brand spanking new, a slight coat of dust covered the frame, but otherwise, it shined like a washed golf ball. Murray tested the hand brakes. They squeaked from disuse, yet gripped the tires firmly. Murray double-checked the chain. Everything appeared to be in riding condition. On your mark… Get set…

Murray climbed onto the black banana seat. His feet touched the ground as if the bike had been custom-built for him. He took a deep breath, kicked up the kickstand, and pedaled down the driveway. He looked both ways for traffic. The boulevard basked in silence and sunshine. Murray pumped the pedals and hopped over the curb.

Cab grinned from the porch. "And no Evel Knievel stunts!"

Butterflies filled Murray's stomach as he took off down the street. The warm wind tousled his hair and made him long even more for the lakeshore. He had yet to travel up to this end of the block. His eyes locked on Ms. Crestwick's house next door to Cab's. She lived in a lavender rambler on a short green lawn landscaped with white rocks. Pink and white carnations bordered the length of the property line. A hawthorn towered in the center of the yard, its branches weighed down by white flowers and reddish fruits. Murray wondered briefly if Ms. Crestwick befriended the neighborhood hags.

Three loud barks startled Murray. The bike wobbled as he looked over his shoulder. The Rottweiler returned to reacquaint himself, without a leash to hold him back. He sprinted from the shadows of Mr. Havlock's front yard. Murray's instincts told him to pedal faster. He pumped his legs hard out of the coast.

Mr. Havlock rounded the corner of his house, hiking his brown suspenders over the straps of his stained tank top. "Pontius! Get back here!"

The command fell on deaf ears. Pontius locked his sights on the bike, barking in pursuit like a cop car and siren. Murray pedaled like mad down the boulevard. Reluctant to look back, he knew the hellhound neared by the distinct sound of his paws kicking up loose rock.

Cab rushed down his porch steps. "Dammit, Havlock!"

Murray glanced over his shoulder. Pontius snarled and snapped at the rear wheel, missing it by inches. Murray looked ahead. The end of the block approached fast. Cab had been adamant about remaining on the boulevard.

Without even looking both ways, Murray barreled into the intersection of Lazarus Lane. Pontius pounced like a puma.

Murray cranked the handlebars sharply to pull a U-turn. The rear tire skidded across the rocks. Pontius snapped at air and landed a few feet past the bike. Murray jumped at the opportunity to break away.

A spine-tingling screech resounded through the neighborhood. Murray glanced back in time to see a black hearse slam into Pontius. The Rottweiler yelped and flew a good twenty feet before thudding down in Mr. Havlock's front yard. Murray braked hard and skidded to a stop.

Mr. Havlock ran to his baby's side. "Pontius! No!"

Murray stared in shock at the bleeding dog. Sprawled on the grass, he convulsed, eyes wide and glassy. He whimpered in Mr. Havlock's arms. Murray's heart hammered in his ears. He couldn't believe how fast it had all happened. One minute he rode his bike, the next, an attempt at murder and vehicular homicide.

"Murray! Are you okay, son?"

Murray looked down the boulevard and saw Cab jogging toward him.

Wild-eyed and red-faced, tears streamed down Mr. Havlock's haggard cheeks. "Hold on, boy! Hold on! Why the hell are you all just standing there?"

Murray broke his stare and noticed that Mrs. Vitikin and Mrs. Muldoon stood on their doorsteps. Both women simply turned their backs and returned to their houses, as if nothing more than a fender-bender occurred.

Cab reached Murray, huffing and puffing. He placed his hand on the bike for support. "Did that mutt get a nip on you?"

Murray looked at Pontius. Mr. Havlock cradled his lolling head. "No. I'm okay. Don't you think we should call an ambulance?"

"Not for a dog. Besides, that was well-deserved."

"Is it dead?" a deadpan voice asked.

A tall, middle-aged man dressed in a black suit and matching tie approached Mr. Havlock. He stroked his black goatee as if in deep thought about the situation at hand.

Mr. Havlock looked up, eyes afire and bushy brows knitted to the bridge of his nose. "You!" He set Pontius's head down on the bloodstained grass. His eyes landed on Murray. "And you! *Anna's boy!*"

The funeral director took a step forward. "Mister Havlock, involving the police would be unnecessary."

Mr. Havlock leered at the hearse's driver. He stood as tall as his hunched back allowed, yet still a foot shorter than the undertaker. "Your life is unnecessary!"

Cab barged between the two men, hoping to deter an altercation. "If you want, Harvey, I'll help you put her in the hearse. It'd be my pleasure."

"I'll put you in the hearse!"

Mr. Havlock made to charge at Cab, but he tripped over Pontius's leg. He landed flat on his face with a grunt. The funeral director stepped past Cab and offered his hand. Mr. Havlock seized it, pulled himself up, and threw an uppercut with his free hand. The undertaker leaned back out of reach.

Cab intervened once again and shoved both men back to their original places. "Get in the house, son. Now!"

Murray took off on the bike without a second thought. Reluctant to challenge Cab's authority, he sure didn't want to hang around to see Armageddon. He stared straight ahead and pedaled like the spokes were on fire.

Mr. Havlock shook his fist. "You'll pay for this, boy! You and your grandmother!"

Murray coasted up Cab's driveway and parked the bike against the porch. He plopped down on the steps and caught his breath. He gazed across the boulevard to Mr. Havlock. The codger knelt beside the still Rottweiler; blood trickled down the curb like rainwater to the sewer. Murray lacked an ounce of compassion for either man or dog. It felt so wrong, but both entertained cruel intentions. Karma crept up on Pontius; if only the same happened to Mr. Havlock before it was too late.

Murray watched Grandma Anna's Park Avenue turn on-to Blossom Boulevard. He felt nauseous. He wondered how she would react when he told her about his day. His mom, always understanding, gave him the benefit of the doubt. But what if Grandma Anna blamed him for the accident? Would he be sentenced to a life-grounding with no oppor-tunity for parole? Possibly. Heck, he might be better off con-fined to the house at this point.

His gaze wandered over to Mr. Havlock's house. A dark bloodstain on the lawn's edge served as a reminder of the afternoon's events.

Grandma Anna parked in her driveway. Paranoid, Murray glanced to Mrs. Vitikin's house. The front door opened. Mrs. Vitikin nonchalantly put her broom to work on the door-step. Murray's eyes darted to Mrs. Muldoon's place. Oddly, she was nowhere in sight. He half-expected the two busy-bodies to rush over and blurt their juicy gossip. Maybe they were waiting to see if more drama would unfold.

Grandma Anna climbed out of the car and headed across the street with a black hardbound book in hand. She smiled when she reached the bottom of the driveway. "Gentlemen. How was our day? Did we stay out of trouble?"

Cab set his iced tea down and stood from the chair. "Hi, Anna. Oh, not exactly. Old Pontius was off his leash again."

"You're kidding me? Is everyone okay?"

"He tried nippin' at Murray alright."

Grandma Anna followed the walk, eyeing the bike near

the porch for a brief moment. She regarded Murray as he stood on the steps. "Are you hurt?" Murray shook his head. "Well, that's the last straw. I warned Havlock yesterday. That dog will be put to sleep after I'm through."

"I don't think there'll be a need for that."

"Why not?"

"Go ahead, son. You might as well tell her what happened. Hearin' it firsthand is always better than second."

"The truth, at any rate. Well? C'mon. Spit it out."

After a moment of thought, Murray chose his words carefully, uncertain how Grandma Anna might react. "After lunch…and watching the baseball game…I went for a bike ride."

"Bike ride? Whose bike?"

Cab leaned against the porch railing. "My grandson's bike. It's Murray's now. If that's alright with you."

Grandma Anna half-turned and eyed the bicycle. "Fine. So what happened?"

Murray pointed at Mr. Havlock's bloodstained lawn. "I was riding down the street. And Pontius started chasing me. I spun out on the corner…and a car came…and ran into him."

Cab grinned. "A hearse."

Grandma Anna raised her eyebrows. A ghost of a smile crossed her face and faded like winter breath. She shook her head and looked at Mr. Havlock's house. "So how's Pontius?"

Cab crossed his arms. "Dead. Havlock's crushed. Took off in his car a while ago. I'm guessin' he won't be back 'til dark. He must be sick of bein' on our radar screen."

"Good heavens. I can't even leave you two alone for one day."

"I didn't do anything wrong, Grandma! I swear!"

"I know, Murray. And even if you had, I hate that mutt with a passion. Now that he's at peace, so is the whole block."

Cab straightened, stretched with a groan, and changed the subject. "So, Anna, whatcha got there? Homework?"

Grandma Anna handed the book to Cab over the railing. "More like the reading material you wanted. When are you going to get your own library card?"

"Probably when yours gets revoked. Thank you kindly, Anna. I know how I'm goin' to spend the rest of my summer."

"Thank you for keeping an eye on Murray today. It's nice to know I have one neighbor I can trust."

"Anytime. I enjoyed myself. How 'bout you, son? Hope I haven't scared you into not comin' back."

Murray smiled. "Not yet. There's always next time."

Anna placed a hand on Murray's arm and guided him off the steps. "See you tomorrow, Cab."

Cab leaned over the railing. "Make that Friday. I'm headin' up to my cabin for a bit."

"Bigfoot hunting again?"

"Ha! I think if I saw a yeti I'd ask it to go fishin' with me. I'm trustin' Murray will hold the fort down?"

Murray half-smiled as dread washed over him. What would he do without his only friend around? The one person who shared an understanding? With Cab out of the picture, the hags would definitely be brewing ill will. Murray felt the target on his back.

He nodded. "Can I take the bike with me? I might get bored."

"It's yours to keep. But if I get back and the whole block's in flames, I'll be knockin' at your door."

Cab chuckled as Murray and Anna said their goodbyes and headed across the street. Murray honed in on Mrs. Vitikin's bay window. The curtains swayed as if stirred by air conditioning, but Murray knew otherwise. Mrs. Vitikin had been watching all along.

❈ ❈ ❈

Twenty minutes later, Grandma Anna packed the picnic basket with jelly sandwiches, Cheetos, and Coca-Cola. She insisted Murray dress warmer, even though it was almost eighty degrees outside, assuring him it would be a lot chillier by the lake. Not about to argue, he burned to see Superior, so he hurried to his room and returned to the kitchen in record time wearing a pair of blue jeans and a green sweatshirt.

Grandma Anna slipped on a gray sweater over her blue turtleneck. "All set?"

"I am if you are."

"Indeed. Then we're off."

They headed out to the Park Avenue and drove off. Murray bubbled with excitement. Finally, he would see the lake, not to mention downtown Windom. They turned left onto Lazarus Lane.

Grandma Anna broke the comforting silence. "Sweetie, if I ask you something about today, will you tell me the truth?"

"Of course."

"Was Cab in the house while you were riding your bike?"

"Uh-uh. He was outside watching me."

"Good. I thought so. I should've known better than to listen to Missus Vitikin."

"You talked to her already? We weren't even home half an hour."

"She called while you were upstairs. Believe it or not, she's my eyes and ears. So if you're ever up to trouble while I'm at work, she'll be quick to tell me."

Murray gaped at Grandma Anna. He could not believe what he just heard. In so many words, Mrs. Vitikin babysat him at the same time as Cab. What else was Mrs. Vitikin asked to do? Keep a log of every time Murray stepped out of the house? The paranoia ate at him.

He looked away and gazed out the passenger's side window. Town Curve wound along the sheer bluffs. Kay's Cafe's red awnings and sandstone walls gave it the look of a giant Cracker Jack box. The supermarket next door looked like an Old West general store, complete with a redwood porch and five-foot totem pole mailbox. Farther along the bend sat the ivied brick post office and quaint library shaped like a bookend. It was the strangest downtown Murray ever saw.

He pointed out his window. "Is that the library?"

"The one and only. And you know, if you ever want me to check you out some books, I'd be happy to."

Murray nodded. "Where is the nursing home?"

"About ten minutes outside of town. Not too far from here."

His mind dwelt on the cafe and Saturday breakfasts with his mom. "What about the cafe? Could we eat there sometime?"

Grandma Anna smiled. "Sick of my cooking already? So am I. Luckily, it's French Toast Thursday tomorrow. Kay had better save us a booth."

Grandma Anna winked as downtown shrank away. The Park Avenue coasted past Windom Methodist Church. Off-white with limestone steps and a spire belfry, it loomed over a grove of birches. The skyline looked like a Martian landscape; jagged bluffs pierced the fiery horizon.

Murray wondered where the lakeshore started. They passed the bluffs a few blocks back, so it must be close. "Are we almost there?"

"Just about. See that glint off to the right?" Murray squinted into the distance and nodded. "That's the silk lanterns. They decorate the dock posts every summer."

The Park Avenue traveled the stretch of road and turned into a gravel lot. They parked near a brick sidewalk and climbed out.

Grandma Anna opened the trunk. "You get the blanket, and I'll get the basket. Deal?"

"Deal."

Murray put the pink-flowered blanket in the crook of his arm as Grandma Anna grabbed the basket and shut the trunk. They walked side by side to the walk.

Grandma Anna gestured ahead. "I know the perfect spot for a picnic. This way. Just off the boardwalk."

They followed the walk downhill where the birches receded and the ironwood boardwalk mingled with the lake. The magenta horizon reflected off the sparkling water, resembling pink lemonade. The brisk breeze nipped Murray's cheeks, making him glad he ditched his shorts and T-shirt for blue jeans and a sweatshirt.

Grandma Anna stopped at the foot of the boardwalk and pointed toward the lake. "We'll go to the lookout before we leave. It's simply breathtaking in the evening with the lanterns lit and the moon shining. Sound like a plan?"

"Yeah. I can't wait 'til the sun sets."

"Me neither. C'mon."

They stepped off the boardwalk and headed down a flight of stairs that led to a grassy knoll. There, a towering maple cast a shadow on the rocky shore. Grandma Anna set down the basket. Murray handed her the blanket.

She laid it out beneath the canopy. "Have a seat!"

Murray sat down and gazed at the lake as Grandma Anna unloaded the basket. Superior was everything he imagined, sparkling, endless, like looking at an ocean. He could see a speck of land in the distance, but otherwise only water. Toward the west, a steamship inched past the setting sun. A scattering of yachts drifted in the east, probably having their own picnic. Murray took a deep breath of the fresh air and felt the troubles of the day wash away in the tide.

Grandma Anna set a paper plate before Murray with a jelly sandwich and Cheetos on it. "You know, your mother and I used to come down here all the time. She loved it at night. The lanterns, the ships, Split Rock."

"How come she left, Grandma?"

"I ask myself that all the time, Murray, and I never come up with the same answer twice. Maybe I was too strict with her. Maybe she couldn't stand watching Grandpa Macon drink himself to death. Or maybe it was the only way to escape this town. I personally think all of the above."

Murray grabbed a Cheeto, hoping to shed more light on his uncertainties. "How long has Grandpa Macon been gone?"

Grandma Anna's eyes glazed as she looked out at the lake. "A long time, but it seems like yesterday." She paused, lost in the past. "How about a toast?"

Murray grinned as Grandma Anna handed him a Coke. He popped the top, and they both raised their cans.

Grandma Anna smiled. "To our new life together and the times we shared with your mother, my dear daughter. Cheers!"

"Cheers!"

Chapter 5

Grandma Anna sighed as she sipped her cup of tea. "So what are your plans today?"

Murray shrugged. "I don't know. Don't you have to work today?"

"Nope. It's Macon's day today. My plans are laid with him. You're more than welcome to join me."

"Where are you going?"

"Windom Bluffs. Where your grandfather's buried. Unless you'd rather stay home alone."

Murray's fork of French toast paused in midair. The thought of the neighbors spying on him turned his stomach. "I'll go with and keep you company."

"I'd like that."

Murray leaned back in the cafe booth and gazed beyond the awning. The craggy bluffs looked like rusted anchors against the lake and blue sky. Murray's mind drifted with the rolling tide. This would be his second visit to a cemetery; the last one soaked by rain and tears. Regardless of the cloudless sky, he felt the day would be gloomy. He never knew his grandpa, though he tended to believe the man did something to make his mom leave home, something terrible enough to discourage her from returning. With the truth buried six feet deep, he would need to be there for Grandma Anna. After all, she said Grandpa Macon's death seemed like yesterday. To Murray, his mom's funeral seemed like a lifetime ago.

The Park Avenue coasted through the dense mist on Philodendron Drive. Before long, the surroundings changed. The lush maples dissipated as overgrown willows swallowed them whole. The worn road transitioned to a smooth, less-traveled pave.

Murray rolled down his window. He heard the leaves rustling in the warm wind. He never saw so many willows in one spot. "Cool."

"Wait until we come to the cemetery. This time of year the trees are eaten alive by the viceroys."

"Viceroys?"

"Butterflies. They look like monarchs. Sometimes there's so many you can't even see the road."

"Really?"

The Park Avenue decelerated and crawled around the corner onto Willow Pass. The street failed to differ from the others in Windom; it possessed a distinguishing look all its own. The vibrant green trees tapered off to black willows easily thirty feet tall. Sickly looking, they hugged the curb as if fearful of falling down. Open wounds from cankers and borers riddled their branches and black bark. The light mist skittered across the street like ethereal squirrels.

Seconds later, the road came alive. Hundreds of viceroys emerged from the mist and took flight around the Park Avenue. Murray cranked up his window as a brief orange-and-black blizzard battered the car. Grandma Anna smiled at his reaction. Wide-eyed and agape, he watched the butterflies flock to the nearby trees for more feasting.

Murray's heart pounded. "Wow. I thought they were gonna attack us."

Grandma Anna chuckled. "Attack of the Killer Butterflies?"

Murray laughed at the ridiculous thought. Still, the butterflies devoured their surroundings. What if they grew tired of tree bark and acquired the taste for human blood? Anything seemed possible in Windom.

The Park Avenue neared another bend in the road where the mist thickened to a pall. Visibility shrank to no more than a few yards.

Grandma Anna clutched the wheel as she leaned toward the dashboard. Her eyes darted about the mist. "I always dread a deer's going to jump out. Or that I'll crash the gate. And it doesn't matter what time of day you come. It's always like this."

Murray squinted ahead. A dark shape pierced the mist. Grandma Anna brought the Park Avenue to a screeching halt. Six feet from the bumper stood a pair of tall iron gates, the posts corkscrewed and rusted with a "W" on their topsides.

Grandma Anna opened her door. "Darn gates are never open. Wait here."

Murray watched Grandma Anna lift a latch and tug the shrieking gates open until they banged against their posts. She marched back to the car and plopped down in the driver's seat with a huff.

She removed a handkerchief and dabbed her brow. "Either the gates are getting rustier, or I'm getting older."

"They sound like they haven't been opened in a while."

"It makes you wonder. I know they get opened at least

once a year."

The Park Avenue crept through the gates. The paved road crumbled away to gravel, and the sickly willows fanned out into the forlorn cemetery. The mist spilled across the crabgrass and swirled around the numerous weathered tombstones. A plump crow cawed as it glided over the grounds, perhaps acting as the alarm system.

The Park Avenue stopped as the road faded away, swallowed by the mist and dying trees. Murray and Grandma Anna stepped out of the car. An icy gust rocked Murray in mid-stride, carrying the fresh scent of Superior. He gazed at the twisted grove in the distance. He knew the lake lied nearby, and it seemed way more serene than hanging out in the cemetery.

He shut his door. "How far is the lake?"

Grandma Anna pointed over the roof. "The bluffs are just past those trees. Give it a look-see if you want. I won't take it personally. You never knew your grandfather."

"Are you sure?"

"Don't worry, sweetie, we're the only ones here. The gates were shut. And until today, I used to come here by myself."

Murray shook off the willies at the thought of Mrs. Vitikin or Mrs. Muldoon tailing them to the graveyard. After all, they left the gates open for the next visitor. Murray glanced over his shoulder. The road was vacant as a dead man's stare.

Grandma Anna shut her door. "I'll be over by that lamppost." She pointed left at a black pole and lantern amidst the tombstones. "And do me a favor. Don't linger. I don't want you out of my sight for more than a few minutes. Understand?"

"Yeah. I'll find you."

"I hope so."

Murray ran off through the foggy cemetery. Every five paces he dodged a tombstone. The more ground he covered, the softer the crabgrass beneath his feet became, often sinking like mole tunnels. He glanced back. Grandma Anna crouched at a gravesite near the lamppost. Satisfied he lacked a stalker, Murray entered the grove. Wounded as the rest of the trees on the main road, the black willows here differed in one aspect: nodules in place of branches, as if someone had sheared them. It seemed odd to prune trees no one could see. What would be the point? Maybe someone simply created a wider path to the lake. If so, it must have been a nice scenic overlook.

Murray stumbled out of the grove. He came to a four-foot-tall cobblestone wall and an iron lamppost with a dangling lantern. The distant sound of roaring waves reached his ears. He approached the wall and leaned over. Hundreds of feet below, the lake tide crashed against the jagged bluffs.

"Come here often?"

Murray spun on his heels, nearly jumping out of his skin at the frigid voice. A tall man with a black goatee and matching suit smirked from the grove's edge. Murray immediately recognized him as the undertaker who ran down Pontius. Even with the gates shut, at least one other person would be at the cemetery.

Startled, Murray struggled to untie his tongue.

The undertaker approached, his shiny black shoes glinting in the sunlight. "Well?"

Murray backed against the wall. "I'm with my grandma."

"That's funny. I don't see her anywhere."

"She's here. I'll call her."

"You'll scare her. And risk her distrusting you to go off on your own, even down the block on that bike of yours."

The undertaker walked to the wall and gazed at the lake, allowing Murray a close-up of his profile. Face pale and long with high cheekbones, his eyes glared hazel, cold and calculating. His cropped black hair with a streak of gray along the hairline made him look vampiric. Murray eyed his thin lips, searching for fangs.

The man turned and met Murray's stare, stroking his goatee. "So who died?"

Murray returned his gaze to the lake, feigning disinterest. "My grandpa. A while ago."

"I'll say. You obviously never knew him." He paused, waiting for confirmation, but received none. "Consider yourself lucky. Macon Macabe was the town drunk."

"How do you know?"

"I'm the only undertaker in Windom. I know everything…about everyone. I'm like the mailman, delivering bodies to the dirt." He faced Murray, leaning against the wall. "The caretaker of karma. You know, I knew I'd get the best of Pontius one of these days."

Taken aback, Murray turned, mimicking the odd man's stance. "What do you mean?"

"That mutt desecrated these grounds on a daily basis." He reached into his suit coat and withdrew a tin humidor. He removed a cigarillo and stuck it in his mouth. "If he wasn't pissing on the tombstones, he was pawing the plots. That accident was long overdue."

"Are you sure it was an accident?" Murray began to think it an act of vengeance.

The undertaker smiled, removed a Zippo, and sparked a flame. He puffed the cigarillo to a steady burn, regarding Murray with an icy stare. "See this?" He gestured at the lamppost. "It's a dark lantern. The panel on the front slides back and forth, hides the light when need be."

"So?"

"So, unless you're sneaking around, there's no need to shut the panel."

Murray's forehead wrinkled, confused, uncertain what the man implied. "I've never been here before. This is my first—"

"Not you." The undertaker tapped ashes over the wall. "The hunters."

Murray looked at him incredulously. He knew a scare tactic when he saw one. Obviously, the man hung out at the cemetery too much. "Hunters?"

The undertaker leaned against the lamppost and took a long drag from his cigarillo. He exhaled a smoke ring "Witch hunters. To this day, they burn them at the stake and dump them over these bluffs."

Murray backed away from the wall and turned to leave. As strangers went, this guy seemed like the type to lure a kid into a white van. "I gotta go. My grandma's probably looking for me."

The undertaker chuckled and flicked his cigarillo into the lake. "So are your neighbors."

"Murray!"

Grandma Anna emerged from the grove, practically colliding with Murray. She halted in surprise and glared at the undertaker. Murray stepped behind her as relief washed over him. He felt like a superhero regaining his strength, knowing his grandmother would defend him.

The undertaker nodded. "Good morning, Anna. Is it that time of year already? It's really too bad you don't come more often."

Grandma Anna's face soured, as if she stood before a landfill. "I'll come whenever I damn please, Mister Talley. See you next year."

"If I don't see you first."

Grandma Anna grabbed Murray by the wrist and led him through the grove. "So what was that man filling your head with?"

"I think he was just trying to scare me. He said witches are burned at the stake on those bluffs."

"Good Lord! He's something else! Always full of horror

stories!"

"It's not true, is it?"

"Of course not. He's an undertaker, Murray. He has nothing but the crows to keep him company. He probably gets a kick out of scaring people."

"Then why aren't there any kids around here?"

"Because they've all grown up and moved on with their lives! Just like your mother did! What in God's name would that have to do with make-believe witches? Goodness gracious!"

Murray let the subject go as they crossed the cemetery to the car. He could not believe he lent an ear to that weirdo. He needed to take a breather and stop worrying about being the only child in town. Of course they all matured and moved on. No conspiracies, just a lot of busybody old folks.

Murray and Grandma Anna reached the car and climbed in. Murray gazed out the passenger side window as the Park Avenue swung a U-turn and followed the road. He kicked himself for not paying his respects to Grandpa Macon, regardless of what Grandma Anna said.

The Park Avenue jolted when it reached the tar, escaping the tendrils of mist groping at the tires. It flew past the gates, which Grandma Anna left wide open, screeching in the breeze.

Murray and Grandma Anna rode in silence until they turned onto Blossom Boulevard.

She flashed a fake smile. "She's finally lost it."

Mrs. Muldoon stood behind the white picket fence with a wooden mallet in hand. Her hair blazed in the wind like a raging campfire. She refused to return Grandma Anna's smile. Rather, she glared and raised the mallet over her head, splitting the picket in two.

Murray did a double take. Her strength alone surprised him. He could not remember ever seeing an old woman mimic a lumberjack. "Why is she destroying her fence?"

Grandma Anna's corny smile failed to falter. "Every so often she replaces the pickets, though usually when she's in a bad mood. You'd think she'd be happy that Cab's out of town."

"Yeah, you'd think."

Murray looked to Mrs. Vitikin's house. There she stood in the shade of a yew tree, clutching her cane in one hand and a claw hammer in the other. "Grandma? Why is Missus Vitikin—?"

"I don't know, but there's Havlock."

Murray looked straight ahead. The Cruiser backed down the driveway and screeched to a halt. Grandma Anna's fake smile faded into stone. Her eyes narrowed like a prowling panther. Her fists opened and closed twice on the steering wheel.

She parked in front of the garage and placed her hand on Murray's leg. "Run along inside."

Murray nodded, perfectly fine with the order. He broke into a sweat as he climbed out, shut the door, and hurried to the front steps.

"Dog killer!"

Murray looked back and saw Mr. Havlock storming across his lawn. His beetle brows united, his yellowed teeth gritted, and his thin hair stirred as if in a cranial dust storm. He balled up his fists. "Anna's boy! Stop right there, goddamn it!"

Grandma Anna tossed Murray the house key. He caught it like a catcher on home plate. "In the house! Now!"

Murray unlocked the door and rushed inside. As he shut it behind him, he glimpsed the boulevard. Mrs. Vitikin lingered in the shadows of her yard. Mrs. Muldoon crossed the street with the mallet in hand. Mr. Havlock approached Grandma

Anna, waving his index finger. Murray ran to the open living room window, crouched down on the couch, and eavesdropped with his letterbox view.

Grandma Anna straightened her back, placing her hands on her hips. "Mister Havlock! I won't warn you again!"

Mr. Havlock stopped a foot from the driveway. "In case you haven't heard, Anna, that little bastard killed my Pontius!"

Grandma Anna kicked Mr. Havlock in the shin. "That little bastard is my grandson! And your little mutt deserved it!"

Mr. Havlock howled, hopping back into his yard. "Now you've done it! Both of you! The day your backs are turned…"

"What? Spit it out! You're going to hurt us?"

Mr. Havlock growled, turned, and hobbled toward his house.

"Anna!"

Grandma Anna whirled and spotted Mrs. Muldoon waddling up the driveway. "Yes, Daisy? Have you come to join Havlock on the ground?"

Mrs. Muldoon stopped within spitting distance. She reached over and set her mallet on the car's trunk. "Actually, I was hoping you'd lend me a bag of apples, hmm? Eveleth mentioned you scored a good deal at the farmer's market last week."

Grandma Anna huffed. "Of course. Let's go inside. I need to cool down."

Murray scrambled off the couch. He ran to the foyer, kicked off his shoes, and ducked into the kitchen. His brain felt like a pinball machine, wondering, calculating, tilting. Mrs. Muldoon was coming into the house! Murray bet she had an ulterior motive. Could it be an attempt to spy on him? Had Mrs. Vitikin put her up to it? And what did she need apples for? Couldn't she go to the farmer's market herself?

The front door opened. Murray grabbed the *Pioneer Press*

off the counter, sat down at the table, and pretended to peruse the front page.

Mrs. Muldoon's voice carried into the kitchen. "So what did Havlock have to say?"

Grandma Anna sighed. "A whole lot about Murray. Hopefully, he'll be saying a lot less now."

"I've noticed he's been in his garage overnight. I'd keep an evil eye on him."

"Trust me. I'll go blind before I stop watching out for him. He's not one to tuck his tail."

Grandma Anna and Mrs. Muldoon entered the kitchen. Murray looked up, still clutching the paper, more out of nerves than continuing his act.

Grandma Anna managed a smile. "Murray, I want you to stay inside the rest of the day. Understood?"

"Okay."

"Have you met Missus Muldoon yet?"

"Kind of. At Cab's yesterday."

"Good. Daisy, I'll be right back with those apples."

Mrs. Muldoon flashed a crooked smile. "Don't be silly. They're still in the cellar, right? I'll save you the trouble."

"Are you sure? I'd say they're five-pound bags. Just be careful on the stairs. The bottom one's got a wobble to it."

Murray gaped at Grandma Anna. He could not believe she would let the crazy ginger roam through the house, especially since she'd swung a mallet five minutes ago. The hag was up to something. She seemed like the type to have a cookbook full of vengeful recipes.

Then it dawned on Murray. *Scorchroaches!*

Murray stood, scooting the chair back. Both women eyed him with raised brows. "I'll go get them."

Mrs. Muldoon leered. "Why? Don't you trust me? Would you feel better if I wore a ski mask?"

Grandma Anna chuckled. "Thank you, Murray, but believe me, it's not the first time Missus Muldoon's ran out of pie filling. That's why I always buy extra."

Mrs. Muldoon smiled, her beady eyes looking straight through Murray. She headed around the corner without another word.

Grandma Anna placed her hands on Murray's shoulders. "It's okay. We've been neighbors for decades. She may seem a little…weird, but she wouldn't hurt a fly."

Murray bit his bottom lip.

"Now, I really need to deep clean that kitchen. Care to help scour?"

Murray managed a half smile. "No, thanks. I'll pass."

"I don't blame you."

Grandma Anna slipped off her pumps and carried them out of the kitchen. The moment she vanished, Mrs. Muldoon appeared around the opposite corner. She held an overflowing bag of apples in her arms. She barged past him and headed toward the foyer. She paused at the doorway and looked over her shoulder. "Murray? Would you be a dear and see me out? I'll need you to open the front door."

Murray hesitated for a second and thought better of it. More than likely Grandma Anna lingered at the front door discarding her shoes, so he would probably just be humoring her. Maybe nicety would return the kindness tenfold. Doubtful, but worth a shot nonetheless.

Murray followed Mrs. Muldoon into the foyer. Grandma Anna's pumps sat before the coat closet, but there was no sign of her. Murray wondered where she went. She definitely trusted Mrs. Muldoon to leave her unattended. Murray shrugged off the thought, brushed past the bag of apples, and opened the door.

Mrs. Muldoon paused at the threshold and faced Murray. Her perfume tickled his nose: an odd blend of frankincense and violets. "Thank you, dear. Let your grandmother know

I'll bring her pie tomorrow." Murray nodded, his hand clutching the knob, eager for her to leave. She lowered her voice to a rasp. "It's no secret. We know what you are."

For a moment, Murray considered slamming the door on her. Instead, he bit his tongue as Mrs. Muldoon left him baffled. He shut the door and locked the deadbolt.

He peered out the narrow foyer window and watched Mrs. Muldoon waddle down the driveway, her head craned around the bag of apples. What a lunatic! She spoke like the Grim Reaper, but the old hag played the Devil in disguise. After the menacing comment, Murray knew she planned to cook more than cobblers. He needed to check the cellar without Grandma Anna getting suspicious.

Truth be told, if scorchroaches milled about in a good dose of moonlight, their house would go up in flames like the Fennely Farm.

✹ ✹ ✹

At dinner, curiosity ate Murray alive. He could not stop thinking about the neighbors. Cab was the only one who had yet to threaten him. And, of course, Ms. Crestwick, who seemingly vacationed a lot. Mrs. Vitikin and Mrs. Muldoon appeared to be partners in crime, while Mr. Havlock topped everyone's hit list. Besides Cab, Murray wondered how many of them had grandchildren. While a scary thought, it might be an opportunity to find common ground. Or they all lived their lives as stone-cold curmudgeons.

Murray swallowed a bite of macaroni and spoke his mind. "Does Missus Vitikin have any kids or grandkids?"

Grandma Anna looked up from her plate. She dwelled on the question as if considering whether to divulge the details. "She has a daughter who pops into town maybe once a year. She had a grandson, but he was put up for adoption when he was born."

"What about Missus Muldoon?"

"She had twin boys. Unfortunately, they died of pneumonia when they were four."

"And Mister Havlock?"

"Havlock? Isn't it obvious? He was an only child. I don't think he ever thought of anyone but himself."

"Miz Crestwick?"

Grandma Anna chuckled. "Oh no. She's too much of a free spirit. When she's not vacationing, she's the life of the party. Youthful, selfless. Believe it or not, she keeps everyone on the block in line."

Murray's mind drifted as his hunger took hold. Ms. Crestwick sounded like someone he could definitely get along with. He failed to believe anyone could keep the neighborhood hags out of trouble, Mr. Havlock included. She must have been quite the diplomat. Still, she lacked grandchildren, too.

Running off his thoughts, Murray set his fork down and looked Grandma Anna in the eye. "How come you never came to see us in Rushford?"

Grandma Anna took a long sip of her wine, her gaze unflinching. "Well, your mother wanted me to keep my distance. I did some things in the past I regret now. Boy, do I ever. But what's done is done. I'm not so certain she ever forgave me." She grabbed her napkin and dabbed her eyes. "When my phone calls and letters went unanswered, I figured it was too late to fix the damage. I respected her decision."

Murray let the conversation drop as Grandma Anna focused on her wine and neglected her dinner. He mulled over what she said. Whatever occurred, festered, unhealed. His mom, being strong-willed, never turned her back on a problem in life. Maybe the pain inflicted was too much for her to bear. Maybe Grandma Anna's dinner would be fossilized by the time Murray drudged up the truth.

He scooped up a forkful of macaroni and did his best to focus on eating. Grandma Anna drained her glass of wine and stood to fetch a refill.

⁂ ⁂ ⁂

When the grandfather clock chimed ten o'clock, Grandma Anna tucked in Murray. Thunder rumbled, sending vibrations through the house. Lightning flashed in fours.

Grandma Anna smiled, noting Murray's worry lines. "You look about as tired as I feel. I promise that tomorrow we'll do something you want to do. I hope you understand why today was different. Your grandfather meant the world to me."

Murray nodded, the comforter tickling his chin. "Like my mom did to me."

"You got it. Now get some rest. And don't worry about the storm; that's all it is, nothing severe." She kissed Murray on the forehead. "Goodnight, sweetie."

"Goodnight."

The moment the light switched off and his bedroom door shut, Murray's thoughts wandered blindly. He recalled Mrs. Muldoon's house call. Images of scorchroaches danced in his head. What if the old hag had planted some in the cellar? One explosion near the furnace and the house would be leveled. Undoubtedly, Mrs. Vitikin put Mrs. Muldoon up to the surveillance task, nosing around Murray, gauging his surroundings.

Lightning flashed like an M240. Thunder rattled the windows.

The storm sparked Murray's conscience, deepening his worry lines. It would only take one flash of lightning to ignite a scorchroach. Even a simple passing car headlight in the window set one off. Murray pictured the vile insects scuttling across the cellar floor.

And that settled it. Murray had to investigate. No way could he sleep knowing scorchroaches might be running a-round the house. He only hoped Grandma Anna had turned in for the night.

He rolled out of bed and tiptoed across the room. The thunder drowned out the groans of the floorboards as the lightning showed him the way. He eased open the door and poked his head into the hallway. A soft glow came from the crack beneath Grandma Anna's bedroom door.

Murray slipped out and quietly shut the door. He crept across the hall, gritting his teeth at every creak, cursing the house for being so old. He stared at Grandma Anna's door, willing her light to extinguish. No such luck. He held his breath as he walked by. The floorboards whined.

Murray exhaled when he reached the landing, relieved her bedroom door remained shut. He squinted downstairs. The lightning strobe cut a path through the darkness. Murray clutched the railing and walked down the steps. These boards seemed to creak the loudest, no matter how soft his foot-fall. Every moment of descent produced a prolonged moan, like he was walking on turtle shells.

He sighed when he set foot in the foyer. The lightning flashes once again helped him navigate. He tiptoed beneath the archway and entered the living room. He dropped to his hands and knees, not about to risk being seen by the Peeping Toms. Mrs. Muldoon probably staked out the house all night with binoculars.

Murray crawled across the carpet. Thunder boomed, vi-brating the lamp on the glass end table. The rain came in a downpour, pelting the windows, sounding like blaring radio static.

Murray took advantage of the noise cover and scrambled

around the corner. He stood and saw he was smack dab in front of the cellar door. Its stained glass window depicted a garden of red and white roses, rectangular borders within borders to one central white bloom. Murray grasped the cold brass knob, turned it, and opened the door. It shrieked as thunder cracked above the rain. A string tickled Murray's nose. He pulled it, and a bare bulb revealed an empty closet with a rack of wire hangers. He looked down at the floor. A spiral staircase disappeared into a dark hole.

Murray felt the storm inside him. His heart thundered within his ribcage. Sweat dripped from his armpits. A cool, dank breeze rose from below and stirred his hair. As much as he dreaded entering the pitch black cellar, his conscience prodded him. He needed to ensure no insect time bombs ran toward the light.

He shut the door and descended the narrow steps. The darkness reeked of must and apples. Murray felt the wall for a switch and, to his surprise, found one. The second an array of bare black light bulbs flickered to life, he chided himself, realizing he could have blown the house sky high with his stupidity. Unless, of course, scorchroaches only reacted to natural light.

He scanned the purple cellar, slightly distracted by the weird psychedelic glow of his striped pajamas. On the left sat a cluster of paper bags filled with red apples. On the right, five six-foot-tall rows of redwood racks containing wine bottles.

A blast of thunder rocked the cellar. The bottles vibrated against each other, sounding like a train was passing behind the house. He glanced back, paranoid the ruckus had roused Grandma Anna. He was alone, though, so he needed to make his search quick. If he were caught red-handed snooping around, the end result might be bad. He turned and eyed the six bags of apples. He dismissed them, not about to sift through each one for a scorchroach. Surely Mrs. Muldoon would have planted it in a more open spot. Murray's eyes darted to the nearest cobwebbed corner. A Daddy Long Legs, but no scorchroach.

He hurried down the middle row of racks. Thunder like a shotgun blast cued the symphony. Murray's heart hammered, certain the bottles would shatter into pieces. At the end of the row, he scanned the back cement wall. Four wooden barrels stood below a foggy rectangular window cracked enough to smell the scent of rain. To the right huddled a gas furnace and water softener, appearing robotic in the black light glow.

Murray's brain spun like a hamster wheel. The furnace. Maybe Mrs. Muldoon planted the scorchroaches there. It would be the easiest way to blow up the house. Murray walked over and dropped down to his hands and knees. He peered beneath the furnace.

Nothing but cobwebs.

Under the water softener.

No scorchroaches there either.

Murray stood and sighed. He began to realize he had overreacted. Mrs. Muldoon simply came to borrow a bag of apples. Just like Cab falsely accused her, Murray felt as if he was in the same sinking boat.

Lightning flashed. Murray's eyes settled on the window. He knew it faced the side of Mrs. Vitikin's house. He grinned. Maybe he could spy on her for a change. He clambered onto a nearby barrel. He stood carefully, his makeshift stool wobbling beneath his feet. He looked up, the window exactly eye level.

Murray wiped his hand across the foggy glass. The storm still carried on. The rain poured down. The wind howled, whipping the trees back and forth. Mrs. Vitikin's house sat no more than ten yards away. A nearly identical foggy rectangular window paralleled the one from which Murray peered. His hopes skyrocketed. He really would be able to spy on her.

He stared at the adjacent window, praying for a glimpse of her. He felt as if he were in a submarine with the periscope raised, watching the enemy. His heart skipped a beat. He squinted, focusing through the rain. Letters slowly formed on the fogged glass, a finger scrawling like chalk on a blackboard. Resulting in a single capitalized word:

HELP

Murray's eyes widened. His jaw dropped, mouth as dry as sandpaper. Mrs. Vitikin caught him playing Peeping Tom. Worry overcame him. The hag would definitely tell Grandma Anna of his spying while he feigned sleep. At which point, Grandma Anna might punish him for sneaking around the house.

Still, the word across the way, condensation slowly dripping, vexed him. Why would Mrs. Vitikin write "HELP" on the window? Help her with what? Did she need someone to call 9-1-1? No, that didn't make sense. Why would she go to the trouble of writing on a basement window at night with a ninety-nine percent chance no one would see it?

Murray stared hard through the rain, convinced he had misread the word. H…E…L…

A hand swiped the cloudy SOS from the window. A sallow face with wild, bloodshot eyes appeared, nose against the glass. Shockingly, not Mrs. Vitikin. It looked to be a young boy around ten or eleven years old. His hair was an uneven rat's nest, almost cartoonish, as if cut with kid scissors. Lightning flashed, and he spotted Murray. His eyes widened, and his jaw slackened in surprise. His face screwed up, and he mouthed—or quite possibly even screamed—"Help me!"

twice.

Murray stood there, frozen and befuddled, struggling to recover from the face slap. Who was this kid? How did he get in Mrs. Vitikin's house? And what in the heck did he need help with?

The boy whirled, and Murray saw the back of his head—bald, marked with a dark smear.

Thunder exploded. Murray jumped a foot in the air, startled. When his feet landed, the barrel toppled under his weight. He crashed down hard on the cement floor, the barrel banging into a nearby wine rack.

He groaned and rolled onto his back. He rubbed his forearms and sat up. Pain shot from his shins to his shoulders. But a second later his aches faded as his brain became distracted. A boy lived in Mrs. Vitikin's house! Yet Grandma Anna said Mrs. Vitikin didn't have any grandchildren. Which could mean only one thing: Mrs. Vitikin had locked the boy in her basement, hidden from the rest of the neighbors. Like a flashcard, the word "HELP" triggered something in Murray. The boy needed help, perhaps to escape the confines of the cellar. Murray had to do something. Thoughts of the evil hag, scorchroaches, and her wielding cane sparked a fire in him. He had to tell Grandma Anna and help the poor little boy who had desperately screamed to him.

He hopped to his feet, wincing, fresh bruises throbbing. He ignored the pain and bolted for the door. The thought of covering his tracks and standing the barrel upright never crossed his mind. He could only think about the captive boy. He blew by the wine racks and bounded upstairs. Out of the closet and crossing the foyer in five seconds flat, the unnoticed strobes of lightning played out his frenzy in slow motion. Thunder drowned his stomps as he ascended the staircase.

He reached the landing and was about to run to Grandma

Anna's bedroom when a light caught his eye. He looked to the left. The trapdoor, left open, emitted a soft glow outlining the spiral steps. Murray recalled Grandma Anna's instructions.

When it's open, you can come up here whenever you like.

Murray took the steps two at a time. He entered the attic, his eyes darting frantically. Three of the windows were cracked open an inch or so, and he smelled the scent of rain mingled with rose incense. The candelabra— relocated to the far side of the room—flickered, determined to stay aflame. The stool remained empty, along with the fresh canvas on the easel. Grandma Anna was nowhere to be found.

Murray's eyes latched on to the black curtain swaying from the rafters. Once again, Grandma Anna's words nagged his conscience.

That's my dark room. It is also the only room in the house you are forbidden to go. Your mother learned the hard way.

Murray thought of the boy in dire need of help. Mrs. Vitikin had locked him in the basement, for God's sake. Surely there were exceptions to Grandma Anna's rule, in case of an emergency.

Murray reached out and drew the curtain aside.

It proved a dark room indeed, windowless and unadorned. Stupefied, Murray struggled to comprehend the structure before him. It looked like something out of a sci-fi movie, such as *E.T. the Extra-Terrestrial.* The creepy scene unfolded in his head. An isolation containment canopy housed a hospital bed with guard rails and an IV pole. Basically, a portable, see-through box comprised of aluminum and clear film. Murray realized it completely inhibited any sickly or medicinal smells from leaking out. The potent candelabra snuffed out any that had managed to sneak through. Within the chamber, Grandma Anna sat near the bedside, leaning forward.

She caught the movement in her periphery and spun,

startled. She stood, kicking the chair back. Murray felt nauseous, his feet rooted to the floor. An old man lay in bed, stock-still, eyes shut.

Murray's brain reeled. *What the heck's going on here? Who is that old man? What is he doing here? And why is Grandma Anna hiding him?*

The entry door to the containment canopy opened, and Grandma Anna slipped out. "Murray! I told you to never come in here!"

He stumbled back, the curtain swarming him. "I… There's a… I was in the cellar, and I—"

"*In the cellar? Now you're in this room! You're supposed to be in bed!*"

"I know, but I… I..." The truth slipped from Murray's grasp. He thought of Mrs. Muldoon and the scorchroaches. He thought of the kid trapped in Mrs. Vitikin's basement. He realized how crazy it sounded. But any crazier than a strange man squirreled away in the attic? "I thought I heard something downstairs. Who— Who is that man?"

"Out! Now! How dare you disobey me!"

"There's a boy in Missus Vitikin's basement! I saw him! She has him locked up down there!"

Grandma Anna scowled, red-faced, livid. "I warned you!"

"But it's true!"

"Enough! I told you not to come in here, and you did anyway!"

"But who is that? Ow!"

Grandma Anna had seized Murray's arm and yanked him through the curtain, nearly tearing it off the rod. His eyes widened with fright. He never saw her so angry before. What was he thinking? He should have gone back to bed. He should never have barged into the room, especially without evidence to back up his accusations. He should have kept his mouth shut. Unfortunately, all said and done, punishment stared him down. Was he being dragged to a corner? Grounded to his room? Whatever the discipline, did he really deserve it for discovering Grandma Anna's weird secret?

She dragged Murray downstairs. "You're the only child in town, and you still can't stay out of trouble!"

"But I'm not the only one! There's a boy! I swear!"

"Nonsense!"

She tugged Murray across the landing and down the hardwood steps. He stumbled into the foyer, nearly causing them both to fall. Fear overtook worry. She jerked Murray into the living room. He winced, nervous and full of dread. What was downstairs she could use as punishment?

Grandma Anna stopped and turned on Murray. Lightning lit up the house as Grandma Anna pointed, scowling. The closet door swung wide open. Thunder cracked. "In! Now!"

Murray shook his head, terrified. Grandma Anna planned to lock him in the cellar, like the boy next door. He spun and attempted to break free of her grasp. She grabbed his other wrist and yanked him forward. He fell to the closet floor. He looked up with a groan.

Grandma Anna loomed over him. "Get down there!"

Murray scrambled to the steps. Grandma Anna snatched a handful of wire hangers off the rack and threw them aside; they clattered against a nearby wall. Murray stood, hunched over, and hurried down the staircase. The spiral disoriented him, and he tripped on the last step, falling face first on the concrete floor.

Pain exploded through his kneecap. He gritted his teeth, jumped to his feet, and lunged back up the steps.

"Grandma! Don't leave me down here! I'll be good! I promise!" Murray heard the door shut and the lock click. "Grandma, please!"

He collapsed on the steps as tears fell. He wished he had never disturbed Grandma Anna. Instead of returning to his bedroom and sleeping it off, he had overreacted. He had disobeyed the house rules and ended up in solitary confinement.

The storm cast a brief nightlight, soon swallowed by darkness, like a torch extinguished in a cave. Thunder rumbled, clinking the wine racks as if in a toast. Murray buried his head in his arms and stretched out across the stairs. He cried while the rain poured harder, eventually lulling him to a restless sleep.

Chapter 6

Murray stirred from his slumber. He dried his eyes on his pajama sleeves and rose from his huddle. He sat on the steps, adjusting his eyes to the darkness. He scolded himself. Short-tempered and deaf to reason, Grandma Anna was nothing like his mom. She always took the time to discuss a problem before she handed down punishment. Even then it was minor, a week without TV or confinement to his room for two hours. Grandma Anna seemed more like a stick of dynamite, itching to blow her top.

Murray stood as the cellar solidified into dismal silhouettes. He reached over the railing and felt the wall for the light switch. He found it and flipped it. Nothing. He flipped it again. Still no response, not even a flicker of phosphorescence. Murray figured the storm had knocked out the power. The darkness made his skin crawl. He could not stop thinking about spiders and centipedes and roaches.

Scorchroaches!

Thoughts of the captive boy resurfaced. Murray left the steps and stumbled forward into the darkness. Thunder rumbled low in the distance, too weak to commence its Merlot symphony. Murray reached his arms out blindly, searching for reassurance. He soon found himself wandering between two racks. His hands ran along the bottles, tingling at their coldness and coating of dust. The darkness lightened with each step. The racks disappeared altogether, and his hands fell to his side.

He looked up at the window. The outside light seemed faint, but brighter than his surroundings. He spotted the up-ended barrel. He stood it upright, surprised by its light weight, and pushed it back to its rightful place. He carefully climbed atop, reminding himself not to make any sudden moves or he would lose his balance. His curiosity burned. He yearned to help the boy.

He leaned over the cobwebbed sill and squinted out the smudged glass. The rain had let up, reduced to a dying sprinkle. The window across the yard was dimly lit and empty.

Murray wiped the dust off the glass for a better view. The barrel rocked beneath his feet. He glanced down and widened his stance. When he looked back up, the boy's gaunt face once again appeared in the parallel window. Startled, Murray clutched the sill for support as his knees weakened. The boy looked terror-stricken, still wild-eyed and cranking his head over his shoulders every second. His small hands trembled against the glass. He mouthed two words slowly, enunciating them for an amateur lip reader. Murray understood them perfectly: "Help me!"

He unlocked the window and shoved it. Surprisingly, it creaked open, just wide enough to poke his face out. Murray was about to yell across the way when the boy ducked out of sight.

Murray sighed, frustration setting in. One second the kid was begging for help, the next he wanted to play hide-and-seek.

"*Over here!*"

Murray leaned back from the window, hunkered down, and peered over the sill. He pricked his ears at the urgent whisper. Two shadows passed between the houses. They stopped beneath a nearby apple tree, maybe ten feet from the cellar window, in a shaft of moonlight. The tall woman was Mrs. Vitikin, clad in her typical black dress and shawl. Murray eyed her counterpart and crinkled his forehead. He expected to see one of the neighbors, Mrs. Muldoon or the elusive Ms. Crestwick. Instead, a much younger, dark-haired woman in a sleeveless white dress with lace stitching stood across from Mrs. Vitikin. Her skin seemed to glow, and her thin red lips glistened like wet strawberries. Both women glanced around, ensuring they were alone. Their hushed conversation carried clearly on the breeze.

The young woman spoke in a soft, seductive tone. "Has the cordial been brewed?"

Mrs. Vitikin raised her chin in an almost obedient manner. "The blackthorns are boiling in the cider." She outstretched her hand. "The burnt betony."

"Your merit for Moloch."

"And the rosary?"

"Gather the bloodroot and hemlock off Willow Pass. Inform Daisy to prepare the passage."

Mrs. Vitikin nodded. "The nymphs will be adults by Morrigan's moon."

The young woman plucked an apple from the tree and caressed it with her ringed finger, the emerald glinting in the light. "And our host?"

"We may have two. The Macabe boy."

"You're certain he's immune?"

"Trial by fire."

"Wonderful news indeed. I fear the hunters are closing in."

The apple surged red in the young woman's hand. It split

apart and bloomed into a pink rose, the rind peeling into petals. The stemless flower hovered over the woman's open fingers, rotating amidst a nebula of something like pollen and pixie dust.

She raised her hand and spit on the rose. It blackened and withered, crumbling to ashes. The young witch blew the remnants—along with the nebula—into nothingness, like a firefly blinking out.

She raised her finger to Mrs. Vitikin's lips. "When slumber falls and the progeny blood spills, our savior will awaken and bless us with their immunity. Now be off, before the moon gives me cause to conjure."

Murray watched the women shuffle into the night. Even after they disappeared, he still stared after them. What had he just witnessed? And who was the young woman? Murray felt a headache forming at his temples. Maybe the stress of the evening had jaded him. After all, there were no such things as magic and…witches.

Murray's trance shifted to the parallel window; it was vacant and childless. Mrs. Vitikin was a witch! Did Grandma Anna know? Or did she practice witchcraft, too? Based on the conversation, Mrs. Muldoon definitely stirred the cauldron as well. But what about Mr. Havlock and Cab?

Murray closed his eyes, sat down on the barrelhead, and leaned against the cement wall. His brain hurt. Magic or no magic, Mrs. Vitikin and the strange young woman schemed. Their cryptic conversation confused Murray, but why else would they meet so secretively, and whisper on top of that? And what did they plan on doing? Something to the boy in the basement? And worse yet…

They know that fire doesn't hurt me!

Murray put two and two together. The scorchroach. A trial by fire. And another possessed his weird gift. Grandma Anna? Or could it be the boy locked in the basement?

Murray attempted to open his eyes, but in the end, he relented to exhaustion. His body went limp and slumped on the barrel as the breeze coaxed him, tousling his hair through the window.

⊗ ⊗ ⊗

The roar of a nearby lawnmower snapped Murray back to consciousness. His eyelids fluttered, correcting the bright blur of the cellar like an optometrist's tool. The rafters and wine racks zoomed into focus, glinting in the morning light.

Murray rubbed his eyes and hopped down from the barrel. He cracked his sore neck and stretched his arms, his makeshift bed fit for a prisoner. He wondered what time it was. Apparently late enough to mow the lawn and disturb the peace. Murray figured maybe 9:00 or 10:00 a.m. His stomach grumbled. He swallowed and grimaced, his throat parched. He walked sluggishly between two racks. He passed by the paper bags. He briefly considered pausing to bob for apples, but then thought of the repercussions. He had learned his lesson from solitary confinement. He looked up the spiral.

Grandma Anna loomed at the top, hands on her hips, scowling. "It's eight-thirty. Get up here and eat breakfast."

Murray almost played the brat and replied, "I'm not hungry," but instead he bit his tongue and hung his head. He grabbed the railing and headed up. Grandma Anna disappeared. When Murray reached the closet and stepped out, the sunlight blinded him. Squinting and blinking, he entered the kitchen. His breakfast waited for him—a bowl of oatmeal and two slices of toast. Grandma Anna leaned against the counter as she drank her cup of tea. Murray ignored her and plopped down at the table.

Grandma Anna dropped her cup into the sink; it clattered against an accumulation of dishes. "Now that you've had time to think, you're officially grounded. You're not to leave this house or set foot in the attic. TV is also off limits. When you're done eating, I have a list of chores that I want done by lunchtime. Understood?"

Murray nodded. He nibbled his toast; it was cold and limp.

Grandma Anna slapped a piece of paper on the counter. "I will not tolerate disobedience in this house. Next time you'll get the strop and a day in the cellar. Now, where's my apology?"

Murray gulped down a spoonful of lukewarm oatmeal and met her glare. "I'm sorry."

"For?"

"Going in the dark room."

"And?"

"And…sneaking around the house. But who is that—"

"Don't let it happen again!"

Grandma Anna marched out of the kitchen, not about to entertain a Q&A session. Murray set down his spoon and gazed out the window. The sun shined, and the grass glistened from last night's rain. Cab's porch and driveway remained empty. Murray hoped he returned sooner rather than later. Things were spiraling out of control. The more secrets he uncovered, the more suspicious the next-door neighbors seemed.

Last night's magic show materialized in Murray's mind. The swirling nebula. The apple blooming into a rose. The grand finale of ashes.

Murray thought again of the young woman. Who was she? Maybe Mrs. Vitikin's daughter? Grandma Anna mentioned she occasionally came to town. Yet the pieces of the puzzle failed to fit. The likelihood was slim that a daughter would order her mother around, especially when that mother was Mrs. Vitikin.

Murray's memory latched onto the undertaker's odd

statement. *Witch hunters. To this day, they burn them at the stake and dump them over these bluffs.*

What had Mrs. Vitikin's companion said?

I fear the hunters are closing in.

At the time, Murray assumed the undertaker had mastered his scare tactics. Now he wondered if his words rang true.

He scooted his chair back and stood, his appetite gone, along with his freedom. He dumped his oatmeal and toast in the garbage and set his utensils in the sink. He picked up Grandma Anna's list and read it. They were typical chores he had tackled throughout his childhood. Wash the dishes, mop the kitchen floor, vacuum the living room, and dust the foyer paintings.

Murray folded the list in half and shoved it in his pocket. It had been awhile since he'd had to do any chores. The last one he recalled was watering his mom's roses. A wave of sadness and longing crashed over him. He yearned for her comfort, for her to hold him as he cried in her arms. Why did she die and throw him into this crazy life? A tear slid down his cheek. He quickly wiped it away and bit back a whimper. He needed to be strong, just as his mom had always been.

He swallowed the heartache and set to cleaning the kitchen in record time. A half-hour later, the dishes done and kitchen floor spotless, he began emptying the mop bucket when a rap rattled the front door.

He broke into a cold sweat. Grandma Anna toiled in the backyard, beyond earshot, watering her garden. Murray set down the bucket and crept to the window. He leaned against the glass and peered through it. Mrs. Vitikin stared back at him from the steps. Her charcoal-gray dress and black shawl fluttered in the wind. Her dark eyes widened. She raised her cane overhead, intending to pound it against the door. Murray whirled from the window and bolted out of the kitchen. The last thing he needed was Mrs. Vitikin telling Grandma

Anna lies about the other night.

As he rounded the corner and entered the foyer, he slid to a halt. The deadbolt unlocked, and the knob followed suit. Murray's alarm bells sounded. Did Mrs. Vitikin possess a key? Or was she using magic for personal gain? Either way, the devil entered uninvited.

The front door swung open. Murray's instincts urged him to slam it. The angel on his shoulder suggested otherwise, reminding him of Grandma Anna's temper.

Mrs. Vitikin crossed the threshold, and Murray stepped back. The scent of must wafted into the house. "Where are your manners, boy? When I knock, you let me in, not duck and hide. I don't have time for your childish games." She stretched out her hand. "Give this to your grandmother."

Murray gaped at her skeletal fingers, the nails long, yellow, and gnarled. He expected to see a key, but instead she held an odd intertwinement of charred roots and leaves. He immediately wondered what Grandma Anna would want with such a vile necklace. She certainly seemed too classy to wear it.

Mrs. Vitikin scowled and shook her hand, rustling leaves on the floor. "Take it! I'm not getting any younger!"

Murray reluctantly reached for the gift. Mrs. Vitikin brought her cane down hard on his hand, knocking it away like a tree branch. She yanked the necklace over his head and shoved him away with the end of her walking stick. The door slammed shut as Murray fell to the floor, landing on his back. Mrs. Vitikin cackled, a gut-churning rasp and gurgle.

Murray scooted to the staircase. He reached up, clutched the railing, and pulled himself up. His neck burned. A stench similar to tar engulfed him and his eyes blurred. He gasped for air as his head swam. He grasped the necklace, and it shrank in circumference, constricting his throat. His last strands of consciousness slipped away. He staggered aimlessly, as if inebriated, holding onto the baluster for dear life. His legs buckled, and he hit the hardwood face first. His eyes rolled back into his head while Mrs. Vitikin's laughter filled his ears.

The red brick silo rushed toward Murray like a locomotive. A voice rasped from within.

"Moloch, Habetrot,

Morrigan, Tantalus!"

The bricks surged reddish-orange, molten hot, and crumbled to the ground.

Murray gasped, and his eyes snapped open. His head pounded. He blinked hard and strained to focus. He lay on the leather sectional in the living room. Water dripped down his face and off his chin. For the life of him, he had no idea how he ended up there, how much time passed, or what even remotely occurred. His subconscious muddled with the dream; it ebbed and flowed to his temples.

Grandma Anna stood over him, fuming with an empty glass in hand. She grabbed him by the shirt collar and jerked him upright. "*What do you think you're doing? I give you a list of chores to do, and you're napping?*"

Murray opened his mouth, speechless. The recollection revealed itself like a developing print. "I… Missus Vitikin… She was here… She…"

He looked down and felt his throat.

The crude necklace was gone!

Grandma Anna straightened, fists clenched. "I've had it with these lies, Murray! How much do I need to punish you until you learn? You live here by *my* rules!"

Murray sputtered. "I'm not lying! Missus Vitikin was here! She had something to give you!"

"Which was?"

"A necklace."

"Then where is it?"

"I had it. It was here…around my neck. I woke up, and

it was gone."

"Because you were dreaming when you should've been doing your chores! Now get upstairs! I don't want to see you out of that bedroom 'til dinnertime!"

"But, Grandma, she—"

Grandma Anna yanked Murray off the sectional and raised her hand. Sensing a lashing, Murray bolted out of the living room and up the stairs without looking back. He slammed his bedroom door and caught his breath.

His head throbbed, and the questions made it ache more. How had he managed to get himself into such hot water? Grandma Anna refused to believe anything he said. It was all Mrs. Vitikin's fault. And where had the strange necklace gone? The only evidence to support Murray's case vanished as if it were the product of the dream. But he knew it existed. The headache convinced him he'd fallen under the witch's spell. If only he could convince Grandma Anna. Still, she harbored a secret of her own, and she pretended like the incident in the dark room had never occurred. Like there wasn't a stranger sleeping in the attic.

Murray lay down on the four-poster, wishing for aspirin. Remnants of the dream resurfaced. The rushing silo. Red-hot bricks tumbling down.

Murray stared at the ceiling. A bright sunbeam blinded his periphery. He sat up and scooted over to the window, intending to drop the drapes and bask in the darkness. As he undid the sash, he glanced outside. Little could be seen from his vantage point, save for Mrs. Vitikin's parallel upstairs window.

The captive boy appeared across the way. He yelled and beat his small fists against the glass. Murray gaped. The last person Murray expected to see stared back at him. The boy's frantic behavior seemed to indicate an escape attempt. He probably somehow snuck out of the basement, hell-bent on a jailbreak.

The boy looked left and raised his arms as if blocking a punch. Mrs. Vitikin came into view, dropped her cane, and seized him by the wrist. The boy struggled to break free, but she twisted his arm behind his back. The boy lunged at the window, his face slamming against the glass, and Mrs. Vitikin glanced up. Her eyes widened, surprised at her audience, and her scowl curled into a wicked grin.

As she held the boy fast with her right hand, she revealed the crude necklace in her left. She yanked it down over the boy's head and instantly the fight in him subsided. She shoved him aside, bent down, and picked up her cane. She pointed it at the window and jabbed it like a cattle prod, knocking it wide open.

Murray looked over his shoulder, half hoping Grandma Anna would barge in to check on him, but the door remained shut. He knelt on the bed in shock. Mrs. Vitikin reached between her bosom where a wooden whistle dangled. Murray questioned her intentions. Was she going to alert Grandma Anna he was spying? Or summon a flock of Hitchcock's birds to peck him to death?

Mrs. Vitikin brought the whistle to her lips and blew. The breeze turned into a gust and struck Murray's bedroom window. He jumped back in surprise and fell off the side of the bed. He landed on the floor with a thump, flat on his back. He looked up at the window. The glass frosted and icicles crackled down the sill, as if winter had kicked summer to the curb, yet seemingly it was the sole consequence. Murray checked himself over. No frostbite, dizziness, or lethargy. Mother Nature magically drew an ice curtain at the beckon of Mrs. Vitikin's witch whistle.

Murray stood with a wince and rushed to the opposite window. Just as he expected. A snow-free boulevard, summer in full effect. Murray gazed across the room. The ice had melted. The panes dripped in condensation and a puddle formed on the floor. Murray cautiously crept over to the bed. Across the way, the drapes drew on Mrs. Vitikin's window. Murray shook his head, frustrated. He felt so helpless. The witch held a boy captive and probably tortured him senseless. Yet Murray could only watch. He needed to devise a plan to set the boy loose. Before long, Mrs. Vitikin would beat him to a pulp or cast another wicked spell.

Murray returned to the window overlooking the street. Movement caught his eye. Mrs. Muldoon stormed across her yard, hair whipping about like a brush fire. She clutched a black leather pouch in her right hand and her maroon skirt in the other. She appeared to be heading toward Mrs. Vitikin's house.

A car roared to life. Murray looked to the right. Mr. Havlock's Cruiser reversed down the drive and bounced over the curb. Mrs. Muldoon hurried across the boulevard. Murray's eyes widened as Havlock floored it. The Cruiser lunged forward and rocketed past Mrs. Muldoon, brushing her skirt like a bull missing the red cape by inches. She tripped on the curb, stumbled into Mrs. Vitikin's yard, and flipped Havlock the bird. The Cruiser sped off down the block, leaving behind a trail of exhaust.

Murray shook his head as Mrs. Muldoon disappeared from his line of sight, more than likely on her way to help contain the boy. The block was a time bomb; tempers flared and the neighborhood was on the verge of an explosion.

Murray looked down the street. A black Pontiac Sunfire sat in Ms. Crestwick's driveway. It seemed she had returned from vacation. Murray wondered how she fit into the equation. Was she a crazy witch like Mrs. Vitikin? Or kind and caring like Cab?

Murray recalled Grandma Anna's opinion.

She's too much of a free spirit. When she's not vacationing, she's the life of the party. Youthful, selfless. Believe it or not, she keeps everyone on the block in line.

Then he thought of the young woman. Could she have been Ms. Crestwick? No way. Too young. An absence of youth plagued the homeowners on Blossom Boulevard.

While it was hard taking Grandma Anna's word anymore, Murray hoped Ms. Crestwick played the part of peacekeeper. He looked away and stared at Cab's house, wishing he would walk out on the porch with his newspaper and orange juice. Cab gave him the benefit of the doubt. He would listen and relate. He would even advise Murray on how to handle the situation. Boy, he hoped he came back soon.

Grandma Anna entered Murray's room several hours later with a tray of food. He was sitting on the edge of the bed reading an *Iron Fist* comic. He had managed to fight off boredom all afternoon. He'd organized his sock drawer, folded all of his T-shirts, tacked a Marvel collage poster to the wall, and took a nap. In three words: being grounded sucked.

Grandma Anna set the tray down on the dresser, turned to leave, and paused in the doorway. "When you're done with dinner, set the tray in the hall and go to bed. Understand?"

Murray nodded, and Grandma Anna shut the door. He walked over to the dresser. Even though his stomach had been growling for the past hour, his appetite diminished when he eyed the tray. Tuna casserole, canned spinach, and tomato juice. A deliberate meal. Murray hated tuna casserole, and Grandma Anna knew it. Bedtime never sounded better.

Murray grabbed the tray, opened the door, and shoved it into the hall. He shut off the light and crawled beneath the comforter. A shaft of moonlight extended across the room like a macabre catwalk, reminding him of the thunderstorm in the cellar. As flashbacks of the boy and Mrs. Vitikin haunted him, he could have sworn he heard the faint sound of a garage door clacking open as he drifted off to sleep.

Chapter 7

Murray awoke with Grandma Anna's hand on his shoulder. She smiled. "Rise and shine, sweetie."

Murray yawned and sat back against the headboard.

"Why don't you get dressed? I'll have breakfast ready when you come down."

"Okay."

Grandma Anna left, and Murray climbed out of bed. He changed into a sleeveless shirt and a pair of cutoffs. All the while, he brooded about the day before him. Was Grandma Anna done being mad at him? He hoped so. He was tired of feeling guilty, even though he had been honest from day one. And did he dare press her about the strange man in the attic? He felt like he should until she came clean. That still left Mrs. Vitikin. What would she do when they crossed paths? Cast another spell? Murray was unsure what the hag had done to him the last time. Either the necklace possessed magical qualities or its stench produced a drug-induced sleep.

The conversation between Mrs. Vitikin and the unfamiliar young woman came to mind.

"And the rosary?"

"Gather the bloodroot and hemlock off Willow Pass."

The rosary. Murray knew little about church, but a rosary was some kind of necklace. Bloodroot and hemlock, on the other hand, were foreign to him. Those words, again, rang of witchcraft.

Murray headed downstairs and joined Grandma Anna at the kitchen table. His mouth watered at seeing his bowl of chocolate Malt O' Meal, a blueberry muffin, and a glass of orange juice. He sat down and stuffed his face like a rescued prisoner of war.

Grandma Anna nibbled on Melba toast. "I hope after yesterday we're on the same page."

Murray nodded, eyes locked on the table.

"Good. Now I think we both have some explaining to do."

Murray stared at his cereal, wondering what to say. The truth had landed him in the cellar, and obviously, Grandma Anna would not turn on her closest neighbor. Unless she turned a deaf ear because of her anger. Possible, though Murray refused to take any more emotional risks. He had no choice but to concoct a convincing lie.

Grandma Anna cleared her throat and sipped her tea. "Murray, look at me."

Reluctantly, he met her gaze.

"That man you saw in the dark room… I'm not holding him hostage. It's someone I loved. It's your Grandpa Macon."

Murray felt the spoon slipping from his fingers. "What do you—"

"He never died." She looked down at her tea, returned eye contact. "In fact, I faked his death. It's just an empty grave at the cemetery."

"But why?"

Grandma Anna's face flushed, and tears brimmed as the shame resurfaced. "Remember how I told you he drank a lot?"

Murray nodded.

"Well, he was the town drunk and abusive behind closed doors. That's why your mother left." She paused and drained her tea, a lone tear trickling down her cheek. "One night he became upset with me…and hit me…and pushed me down the stairs. Then he had a stroke. And he's been in a coma ever since."

Murray was befuddled. While the story made sense, why all the secrets and lies? Why not let his mean grandfather die and move on? "How come—"

"How come I'm keeping him alive?"

Murray nodded.

"I loved the man that was sober. At the same time, I knew the town would be happy if he was dead. Morally, I knew I couldn't pull the plug. So I faked the whole thing, put the life insurance in a nest egg. Now here I am, airing out my dirty laundry."

"Will he ever wake up?"

"Possibly. He breathes on his own. I keep him in isolation, more so to hide the hospital smell. I feed him through IVs and get him his necessary medications when needed."

"Medications? How could he get those if everyone thinks he's dead?

"I sneak them out of the nursing home. Quite honestly, it's why I volunteer there. That's also where I got all the other supplies. Now I'm not one to ask people to lie, Murray, but this secret must *absolutely* stay between us. Understand?"

Murray half-nodded and drank his juice, his appetite out the window.

Grandma Anna sighed, a colossal weight off her shoulders. "Now, tell me why you were sneaking around the house?"

Murray's tongue felt like sandpaper. "The storm scared me, that's all. I thought I saw someone in the window and I freaked out. I went to your bedroom first and you weren't there and… Sorry…for breaking the rules."

"Let's call it even. Lord knows my sneaking around and stealing is a hundred times worse."

The doorbell chimed, long and sonorous, like a death toll. Grandma Anna and Murray furrowed their brows in unison. Both wondered who could be visiting so early in the morning and pressing on the ringer so rudely.

Grandma Anna stood. "I didn't see anyone go by the window, did you?"

Murray stared outside. "Uh-uh."

Blossom Boulevard was deserted. Grandma Anna sighed and left the kitchen. Curious, Murray crept over to the window and peered as she opened the front door.

"Eveleth," Grandma Anna said with a tinge of worry. "Daisy."

Murray could see Mrs. Vitikin's shawl flapping in the wind, but otherwise, the troublemakers lurked out of sight, apparently crowding the door. Their exchange, however, drifted to his ears loud and clear.

Mrs. Vitikin's voice was deadpan. "I gather you haven't been out to water your garden? Well, don't bother. Havlock finally came out of his garage last night."

"What do you mean?" Grandma Anna asked.

Daisy's reply quavered. "The son of a bitch went on a rampage. He chopped all my sunflowers down! And my tulips!"

"And reaped your roses like stalks of corn," Mrs. Vitikin added. "Guess what we found on your doorstep? A chunk of grass stained with Pontius's blood." She gave pause. Murray guessed she pulled it out of her pocket like another house-warming gift. "Maybe you should frame it over your mantel."

"So…what now?" Grandma Anna asked.

"Claret's back," Mrs. Vitikin said.

"So I see."

"We'll consult her. Havlock leaves for the cafe soon. That would give us a half-hour to do some dirty work."

"Just let me know if there's anything I can do to help."

The door shut, and Murray bolted back to the kitchen table. Grandma Anna returned, smiled weakly, and sat down.

She noted Murray's questioning gaze. "It seems Havlock is at it again. Missus Vitikin said he tore up my garden." Her eyes smoldered like embers. "The *nerve* of that man."

"Are you gonna call the cops?"

"Heaven's no. They're too far away. Besides which, they won't handle any local disputes. They only come out if there's a tragedy."

Murray nibbled his muffin as Grandma Anna's words hit home. He knew no matter how crazy things got on the block, they were on their own. He envisioned the neighbors running amok, the houses in flames, innocent bystanders bleeding on the street, but still no approaching sirens. As his mom said from time to time, things always got worse before they got better. He knew he needed to act fast. The eye of the storm would be overhead by nightfall.

Murray sat at his desk and stared at the clock. He wondered how long until the hags went about their breaking and entering. Mrs. Vitikin proved a professional at that. No telling what they plotted for Havlock. Murray guessed that whatever the scheme was, it would trump the old man's green thumb vandalism. On that line of thought, something occurred to him. With Mrs. Vitikin's house deserted, it would be the perfect opportunity to free the boy next door. He could only hope Grandma Anna joined the troublesome trio outside. Then he needed enough time to pry open the basement window and pull the boy out of confinement. Where they went after that, who knew? Since Cab was still on vacation, Murray's last resort seemed to be Grandma Anna. Maybe once she saw the boy she would lend a helping hand. Murray crossed his fingers. It would be his last-ditch effort before all hell broke loose.

The bedroom door opened and Grandma Anna poked her head in. "Murray, I'll be outside if you need me. That garden's going to be a thorn in my side. And just so you know, I'm taking the day off work since Cab's not around. Are you staying in?"

"For a little bit. I might come out and help when I'm done."

"That's okay, hon. I'd rather you didn't. I could use some alone time. That garden is my pride and joy. If Havlock's torn it up like Missus Vitikin said, then I'll have a lot of mending to do."

Grandma Anna left and shut the door.

Murray searched the desk's pigeonholes and drawers for tools to use on the jailbreak. He found three and stuffed them in his pockets: a letter opener disguised as a Japanese fan, a pair of metal scissors with a plastic guard, and a box of thumbtacks. If all went well, the items would remain concealed. Like rations, they would only be used in a dire situation.

He cracked open the door and listened. He heard the back door rattle shut. He took a deep breath. His conscience urged him to stay and read comics, mind his own business, but his wall of worry and stubbornness stood tall. He bolted down the hall and flew downstairs. He slipped his shoes on in the foyer and peeked out the window.

The coast was clear. Murray hoped the hags put down the telescopes and binoculars, though more than likely all eyes were on Havlock's house. He nonchalantly walked out the front door.

Havlock's garage door clacked open and his Cruiser roared to life. Paranoid, Murray ducked behind a rosebush, knowing the witches would be flying out on their brooms. He watched between the branches as Havlock backed onto the boulevard, automatically shut the garage, and sped off.

Murray listened to his gut and lingered for a bit. Moments later, the hags poured out of Ms. Crestwick's house. Mrs. Vitikin and Mrs. Muldoon flanked the homeowner like three outlaws heading to the thoroughfare for high noon. Ms. Crestwick stood an inch taller than Evil Eveleth with straight, waist-length silver hair. She was dressed in gray slacks, a black blouse, and a white lace sweater. The three women strolled across the street with a confidence that could strike a mighty oak to the ground.

Murray crouched lower and held his breath. The young woman he saw the other night was definitely not Ms. Crestwick. But then who was she? And where had she come from? She certainly didn't live on the block.

The trio headed up Havlock's driveway, their voices carrying on the breeze.

Ms. Crestwick turned to Crazy Daisy. "How many adults?"

Mrs. Muldoon grinned. "Enough to blow the roof off."

"Your merit for Moloch."

"Let's hope the garage is full of flammables."

Mrs. Vitikin snickered. "Plenty, as of yesterday."

Evil Eveleth removed an oversized black key from her pocket. She raised it to her eye and peered through the hole. The garage door jolted and eased open.

Murray backed away from the bush as pieces of the puzzle began to fit. The witches used magic and objects hand in hand. Murray recalled Grandma Anna's door unlocking on its own, the whistle frosting his window, and the necklace putting him to sleep. So maybe they possessed limited powers, which would explain their passion for scorchroaches.

Murray's recollection flared. Ms. Crestwick's comment sounded familiar. What had the mysterious young woman said?

Your merit for Moloch.

Maybe she was Ms. Crestwick's daughter. More importantly, who was Moloch?

Murray bolted around the corner of the house and hid behind the overgrown apple tree. He peered between the branches, scanning his surroundings. There was no sign of Grandma Anna in the backyard. Murray eyed Mrs. Vitikin's house. The basement window was deserted, and he hoped the boy still hung out down there. He didn't have time to search the house for him.

He dashed across the property line and crouched beside the window. He cupped his hands and pressed his nose against the glass, straining to see beyond the glare and smudges.

The boy popped up in the window. Murray's heart leaped, and he lost his balance, falling on his rear end. The boy looked the same, gaunt and mistreated. His hair still looked ratty and unwashed, his eyes wide with dark circles. A fresh bruise spanned his left cheek.

His skeletal hands pushed on the window frame. "Help me!"

Murray slipped his fingers beneath the splintered wood trim and pulled. Even in a joint effort, the window refused to budge.

The boy pounded his fists on the other side. "Hurry! Before she comes back!"

Murray turned his head, paranoid. Thankfully, there was no one in sight. "Quit shouting, or she *will* come back. Just calm down. I have an idea."

He reached into his pocket and withdrew the scissors. He tossed aside the plastic guard and jammed the blades beneath the trim. He pried at the window with all his might. The frame groaned, still refusing to give way. The boy shoved from the other side. The frame shrieked and snapped. The window flew up and open as if spring-loaded. Murray once again stumbled backward, this time missing an uppercut by inches while the scissors flipped out of his hand.

He scrambled back on his hands and knees. The boy

leaped up and seized Murray's arms. Though he weighed no more than ninety pounds, the human anchor dragged Murray forward, and he realized he lacked a foothold. Before Murray knew it, he toppled head over heels through the window. Easily a seven-foot drop, his fall was luckily broken by a pile of boxes.

He grumbled and coughed, engulfed by a cloud of dust. He stood and looked about. The basement resembled Grandma Anna's, dark and musty with cinder block walls. Except, instead of wine racks, the room was near empty. A single bare bulb flickered in the center of the ceiling. At the far end stood an iron gate, shut and undoubtedly locked. By Murray's feet, drawn in charcoal on the cement floor, were three concentric circles. He turned and regarded the boy. His clothes were tattered rags. He trembled in the corner, crouched on a stained mattress before a water dish, a metal tray of food scraps, and a pail, as if protecting his territory.

Murray took a step forward as the faint scent of waste matter made him grimace. "C'mon! We have to get out of here!"

The boy shook his head, backing into the wall.

Murray fumed. "What do you mean? You wanted my help! If anyone finds me down here, they'll skin us both! Now c'mon!"

The boy shook his head adamantly. "I can't. There's curses. She warned me."

"The heck with her! She can't curse us if she's not here! I'm getting you out!"

Murray began stacking the boxes back beneath the window, but he soon realized halfway through that most were crushed and unsupportable. He jumped up, reaching for the sill. His hands scraped the wall, coming up a foot short.

He turned and eyed the basement again. "Is that gate locked?"

The boy crouched down, trembling. "Cursed. It's cursed!"

Murray ran to the other side, glancing around. The only way out appeared to be the gate. Murray stopped at the threshold and looked it over. No chains or padlock secured it, and there was no obvious indication of a curse, only the boy's affirmation.

Murray grabbed the handle. The gate sparked and sent an electrical jolt through his body, knocking him off his feet. He landed on his back, twitching and trembling, feeling like a dynamite wick burned through his veins. He groaned and lay on the cement for a long moment, letting the pain subside.

The boy kicked over the pail, snapping Murray from his trance. "She's coming!"

Murray rolled onto his side. The boy looked up at the window. The scythe-shaped tattoo on his nape surged and dimmed red like a beacon. He clutched his temples and dropped to his knees.

Murray stood with a groan. The fiery pain dissipated, but his muscles felt sore and his limbs shaky. "Where is she?"

The boy wavered like a Bobblehead. "Close."

"How close?"

"Can't see her… Can only…feel her."

Murray stared at the window. He expected to see the trio pass by at any second. He looked to the makeshift bedroom. The pail was too small to elevate him to the window. The mattress, on the other hand…

Murray grabbed the boy by the wrist, yanked him to his feet, and pushed him aside. "Get up! And stay over there!"

The boy moaned, the tattoo flashing crimson like a muted siren. Tears spilled down his sunken cheeks. "She's so close. And it hurts so bad."

Murray grabbed the twin-sized mattress and dragged it over to the window. "What the heck is that thing on your neck anyways?"

"I don't know. The old lady…uhh… She drew it on me…

with her fingers. Hurry."

"The old lady? Isn't she your grandma?"

"No. I don't know who she is."

Murray stood the mattress on end. It reached the sill and sagged slightly in the middle.

The boy sat down against the wall, embracing the shadows, and hung his glowing neck between his knees. "She's almost…here."

Murray approached the boy. Now knowing he had been kidnapped added urgency to their situation. "Yes! She's coming! Now get over here and climb the mattress! C'mon!"

The boy raised his head. The warning light cast his screwed-up face in blood red, looking devilish. His eyes narrowed, and he growled. "Don't touch me! Leave me alone! When she gets back, I'm going to tell her what you've done!"

Murray was taken aback. What had come over this kid? One minute, reserved and docile, the next demonically possessed. It had to be the witch's mark. Maybe she controlled him remotely. Maybe the mark compelled him to want to stay. Made him forget he had been kidnapped.

Murray offered his hand. "What the heck are you talking about? Let's get out of here!" He reached for the boy's wrist, but he slapped Murray's hand away.

The boy's nostrils flared. "I said don't touch me!"

Murray backed off. He had already lingered too long. Mrs. Vitikin would be returning soon.

Murray turned his back on the boy and walked to the center of the room. "Fine! Don't ask me for help again! You think that witch is gonna let you go? You're stuck here 'til she kills you! I'm out of here!"

He locked his sights on the window. He sprinted across the basement. He made it as far as the middle of the mattress, then his shoes slipped. He flailed for the sill, but his fingers merely grazed the tattered seam. He slid face first to the floor.

The boy chuckled wickedly as he stood. His tattoo blinked out. He grinned, baring crooked yellow teeth. "She's here."

Murray hopped to his feet, the mattress wobbling in his wake, yet still remaining upright. "Darn it!"

He ran back to his starting line. He barely came up short the last time. He needed more speed, that was all, and less butter on his fingers.

The boy emerged from the shadows. "Where are you going? You can't leave me here."

Murray arched a brow. "What? I'm done playing this game. If you want out, then follow the leader."

He dashed full speed ahead, as if competing in a 100-meter dash. He scaled the mattress a foot higher, felt his shoes slide again, and lunged for the window. He grasped the sill and held on for dear life. Grunting, he mustered his strength and pulled his body over the frame.

The boy ran to the window, looking up wide-eyed. "Wait! Wait for me! Don't leave me here! Please!"

Murray wriggled outside, the fresh air reminding him how dank the basement was. He turned back and reached his hand through the window. "C'mon! Run up the mattress! I'll grab you!"

A teeth-gritting shriek echoed from below. It sounded to Murray like a gate opening. He retracted his hand and side-stepped out of view with his assumption confirmed.

Mrs. Vitikin's voice rumbled throughout the basement. "What's going on here? Trying to escape? I told you not to try it again, didn't I? Maybe this time I should break your little legs!"

Murray glanced about. There was still no sign of Grandma Anna or the other busybodies. He ran across the yard, ducking beneath the apple tree, over to the side of the Macabe Place. He peeked around the corner. Ms. Crestwick and Mrs. Muldoon crossed Havlock's driveway nonchalantly. The garage door was shut tight, without a trace of trespassing or breaking and entering. Murray ducked behind his previous hiding spot and peered between the roses. The witches conversed as before, loud enough for the whole block to hear.

Mrs. Muldoon's hair looked like a half-extinguished fire. "I saved five for the meddler."

Ms. Crestwick smiled as she buttoned up her sweater. "Good. And with a shake of the shawl, the town will wake in a nightmare."

"And who will shepherd the sheep?"

"Eveleth has her orders as you have yours. It's a small window of opportunity. Everything *must* be clockwork."

"Yes, it *must*."

Murray watched them cut through Grandma Anna's front yard and cross the boulevard to Mrs. Muldoon's house. He pondered their conversation. He struggled to make heads or tails of it. The hags' cryptic exchange once again seemed laced with plots of witchcraft, which still sounded surreal, regardless of what he witnessed. He wondered what Mrs. Muldoon meant by the "sheep"? The scorchroaches maybe? Or could it be literal, as in a sacrificial lamb?

"Murray? What are you doing in the bushes?"

Grandma Anna stood on the front step with her arms crossed, glancing back and forth from Murray to Ms. Crestwick and Mrs. Muldoon. A pair of pruners dangled in her fingertips.

Murray stood slowly, racking his brain for an excuse. "Nothing. Just…playing Army. Do you need help with the garden?"

"Oh, no, sweetie. I have a lot of replanting to do." She dabbed the corner of her eyes. "He did quite the number on my roses."

Murray stared at the ground, uncertain how to respond. The garden was Grandma Anna's baby. She fed it, sang to it, and covered it up at night. Havlock's vengeance broke her heart.

She opened the screen door. "Run along now. I'll let you know when it's lunchtime."

"Okay."

Murray took a step toward the corner of the house. When the door shut, he paused and reconsidered his game plan. He hoped to run to his bedroom and hide out until nightfall. But now Grandma Anna expected him to play *Rambo* outside the rest of the morning. He knew one thing: it would be wise to stay clear of Havlock's yard. Whatever the end result, it would be ugly.

As much as he wanted to, Murray headed in the opposite direction, back the way he came, his eyes downcast, still weighing his options.

A door slammed.

Murray looked up, startled.

Mrs. Vitikin stormed toward Grandma Anna's yard, her cane stabbing the grass fast and hard. "Explain yourself, boy!"

Murray paled, and his knees felt like buckling. There could be only one reason why the hag pursued him. The boy snitched. Murray wanted to run for the hills, but doing so admitted guilt. Instead, he stood his ground.

Mrs. Vitikin's eyes bulged. Her lips parted and pursed, parted and pursed, as if practicing a verbal tirade. She crossed the property line and stopped a yard from Murray. She raised her cane and jabbed him in the shoulder, knocking him back a step. "What were you doing in my house?"

Murray opened his mouth, but his tongue struggled to spit out a lie, let alone a single word.

Mrs. Vitikin raised her cane overhead. Murray took another step back and winced, the rosebush literally becoming a thorn in his side.

Mrs. Vitikin cocked back her arm as her scowl deepened.

"Answer me! I know you were there!" She grinned wickedly, and her eyes sparkled. "Your grandmother will be quite upset when I tell her."

Murray peeled his gaze off the cane and steeled himself. "Go ahead. Do it. And I'll tell her about my new friend I met in your basement."

"Friend? You have no friends at my house or anywhere else in this town."

"I took a picture of him in your window." Murray bit back a grin at the brilliant lie. He knew the moment it escaped his lips it was a move worthy of checkmate. "I have proof."

Mrs. Vitikin clutched the cane's handle, white-knuckled. Hatred twisted her face. She glared at Murray as if he had uttered a profanity.

"Eveleth!"

Murray followed Mrs. Vitikin's gaze as she turned her head. Ms. Crestwick crossed the street. Mrs. Vitikin brought the cane down like a guillotine. Murray ducked as it swiped through the bush, but caught the shaft in the left shoulder blade. He stumbled forward, and Mrs. Vitikin seized him by the shirt collar. Ms. Crestwick reached her side in seconds. She snapped off a nearby rose and tied it into a knot. Murray lunged toward the grass, attempting to make tracks. The bush behind him rustled and a branch shot out. It wrapped around his ankles, digging its thorns into his skin. He yelped and hit the ground, tangled up.

Mrs. Vitikin regarded her ally. "He was in my basement."

Ms. Crestwick's gaze narrowed. "Is that so?"

"And he says he took pictures."

"Did you search him?"

Murray's mind rifled through a million escape plans. He conducted an inventory of his possessions. He lost the scissors, and the box of thumbtacks was useless in this situation. But one other item he forgot about. He reached into his pocket and withdrew the Japanese fan. He popped out the letter opener like a switchblade. He rolled onto his back and sliced apart the branch.

Ms. Crestwick crouched to grab his leg. "Not so fast!"

Murray swiped at her hand and left a cut across her knuckles. Ms. Crestwick cried out through gritted teeth. Murray rolled over, Mrs. Vitikin's cane missing him by inches, and scrambled to his feet. He flipped the letter opener back into the fan and jammed it in his pocket as he ran across the yard. He racked his brain for a place to hide until the storm passed over. His eyes latched onto his bike resting against Cab's porch, glinting in the sunlight. Escape. He would pedal the sucker all the way to the brambles, where he ought to get a moment's peace to strategize.

Without another look back, he booked it across the boulevard and bounded the curb to Cab's driveway. More than ever he wished his friend returned as he wheeled the bike to the walk. He straddled the seat and glanced at the war zone. Ms. Crestwick and Mrs. Vitikin were hot on his trail, near the street. Worse yet, Grandma Anna stepped out the front door to see what the commotion was all about.

Murray cursed under his breath. Regardless of the circumstances, another grounding loomed on the horizon. He nearly burned rubber when a bronze car turned onto the boulevard from Philodendron Drive. It honked twice as it approached, like a lost goose happily finding its gaggle.

Murray smiled and sighed. His worries began to fade, and his situation seemed less dire.

Cab to the rescue.

Chapter 8

The Cadillac pulled up the drive, and Cab stepped out. Dressed in khakis and a green Polo shirt, he looked like he was returning from a game of golf. The glare off his head momentarily blinded Murray.

Cab lowered his chin and looked over the lenses of his glasses, assessing the situation. "Leavin' so soon?"

Murray shrugged. "I'm kind of in hot water."

"Scaldin', I'd say. Can't recall ever seein' your grandmother on the heels of Claret and Eveleth. So what'd I miss? C'mon, son, spit it out. Quick."

"Missus Vitikin's accusing me of breaking and entering."

"Say what?" Cab scratched his head. "And did you?"

"There's a boy locked in her basement! She kidnapped him and—"

"Whoa, son, slow down. What about this boy?"

"I swear, Cab! You've got to believe me!"

"Alright now. Zip your lip."

The Windom witches approached the Cadillac as Cab shut the driver's side door. Mrs. Vitikin's scowl froze, and her cane speared the ground, leaving scuff marks on the driveway.

Ms. Crestwick fastened the top button of her sweater, busying her fingers. Grandma Anna trailed her neighbors, on the warpath since she left the front steps.

Ms. Crestwick smiled weakly. "Welcome back, Mister Linlith. How was your getaway?"

Cab removed his glasses and hung them on his shirt pocket. "Apparently not fast enough. What's goin' on here?"

Grandma Anna barged between the hags. "That's what I'd like to know."

Mrs. Vitikin raised her cane and tapped it on the Cadillac's trunk. "Your grandson's been sneaking around my house."

Cab grabbed the cane and shoved Mrs. Vitikin back a step. "Hands to yourself, woman! That's a '76 Fleetwood!"

Grandma Anna clenched her fists. "What do you mean 'sneaking'?"

Mrs. Vitikin withdrew the metal scissors. "I mean the little brat pried my basement window open and took a grand tour."

Cab pointed at her accusingly. "He says you have a boy locked down there."

Mrs. Vitikin bit her lip until she drew blood. She sucked the bead and rasped through clenched teeth. "There are no children in my house."

"Why would he lie about seein' a boy? Doin' his homework or his chores maybe. But he says you're hidin' a damn kid in the basement. Is your grandson over?"

Grandma Anna rounded the car. "Murray, get off the bike."

Ms. Crestwick tapped her nails on the trunk, matching Cab's glower, who looked as if he might slap her hand. "Maybe Murray should be under lock and key. We don't need a thief running around our block."

Cab put his hands up in a "calm down" gesture. "Alright, alright. How about we let him speak instead of burnin' him at the stake? Has it been that long since you hens had kids runnin' around?"

Mrs. Vitikin snickered. "Troublemakers, yes."

Murray's grip white-knuckled on the handlebars, he was reluctant to let go. The neighbors had him cornered—even Grandma Anna had joined their side—and more than ever he wanted to take off down the street. Regardless of his admission, they would never believe him.

Grandma Anna seemed to sense his anxiety. "Murray, this is the last time I'm going to tell you. Get off the bike."

Cab rounded the front bumper and put a hand on Murray's shoulder. "Drop the kickstand, son." Murray obeyed and let the bike rest against the porch. "Now, why don't you tell these ladies what you've been up to?"

Murray cleared his throat. He shuffled his feet, aware eight eyes stared at him, like a spider waiting to catch its prey. He glanced around the gathering. Cab winked reassuringly. Grandma Anna flushed. Mrs. Vitikin's scowl shifted to a grimace. Ms. Crestwick raised her chin and narrowed her eyes.

Murray looked down at the walk, sighed, and faced his accusers. "The night of the storm, I saw a boy in Missus Vitikin's basement window. He wrote 'Help' on the glass."

Mrs. Vitikin twisted her cane into the driveway. "Lies!"

"And then the other day I saw the same boy trying to escape from her upstairs window. But she roughed him up and put the sleeping necklace on him."

"All lies!"

Grandma Anna stepped forward an arm's length ahead of the witches. "The necklace? Is this the same one you told me about the other day? The one you said Missus Vitikin put on you?"

Murray nodded, his hopes lifting. Maybe he finally got his point across.

Mrs. Vitikin's glare made roses wilt. "A sleeping necklace? Yes, I put a sleeping necklace on your grandson. They sell them for half-price at the dollar store."

Grandma Anna raised her index finger. "Enough, Eveleth. Murray, did you break into Missus Vitikin's house?"

Murray gulped, steeling himself for the tongue-lashing. "Not exactly. The window was unlocked."

Mrs. Vitikin tossed the scissors down; they thudded on the concrete walk. "Then what did you use those for, you snake?"

Cab stepped in front of Murray as if shielding him from gunfire. "Okay, cool it already. How about we stop playin' *Columbo* and clear the air? Is there a goddamn boy in your basement or not, woman?"

Mrs. Vitikin pounded her cane like a gavel, jaw clenched, mouth tight-lipped. "I told you… There are *no* children in my house. Do you think I'm running a daycare? I'm on the verge of strangling this brat right here."

Ms. Crestwick stepped aside, placing everyone in her periphery. "I think we need to know if Murray stole anything while he was snooping around, not whether or not a ghost boy is haunting her basement."

Mrs. Vitikin gestured with her cane. "Well, thief? Empty your pockets."

"Agreed." Ms. Crestwick presented her slashed knuckles, the blood having dried before it seeped. "We already know he has a concealed weapon."

Cab raised his hands. "How 'bout we stop with the name-callin' and accusations? Did you see Murray in your house, Eveleth? Yeah, he opened your window and poked his head in, and he won't do it again, right, son?" Murray shook his head. "So let's call it even then and mind our own business."

"Call it even, Mister Linlith? The boy cut me and broke open Eveleth's window. If he won't come clean, then I'm calling the police."

"Please do, so I can report you for trespassin' on my property, which I have a whole helluva lot of witnesses, too, thank you very much."

"Anna? Are you just going to stand there or are you going to search the boy? He's your responsibility."

"Claret, we're going to mind our own business now, and so should you. Let's drop it."

Mrs. Vitikin grumbled, biting her tongue.

Ms. Crestwick straightened and placed a hand on Mrs. Vitikin's forearm. "This time. Next time… We'll be paying you a house call."

"What did I miss?"

Everyone turned as Mrs. Muldoon stopped short of the property line, ensuring not to overstep her boundaries.

Mrs. Vitikin turned and marched off alongside Ms. Crestwick, crushing leaves beneath her cane. "False accusations."

Ms. Crestwick wagged her index finger. "Let's go inside and bring Daisy up to speed."

Grandma Anna, Cab, and Murray shared a moment of silence as they watched the trio head for Mrs. Muldoon's house.

Grandma Ann placed her hands on her hips. "Well, I'm not sure what to make of all that."

Cab raised his brow. "You're not takin' their side, are you? All three are off their rockers. Have you noticed how much time they've been spendin' together? They were takin' walks and havin' lunch dates before I took off to the cabin."

"I'm not taking anyone's side. They were just in Havlock's house doing God knows what. He threw a tantrum while you were gone and tore apart my garden."

"I saw Daisy's sunflowers. I gather he did that, too?"

Grandma Anna nodded. "I think we're the only sane neighbors on the block."

"You can say that again."

Screeching tires paused their conversation. Like a tennis match, their heads turned in unison. Mr. Havlock's Cruiser zoomed down the boulevard as if it were a drag strip. He slammed on his brakes, leaving skid marks, and floored the gas up his driveway, scraping the undercarriage on the curb. His garage door opened automatically. Murray held his breath, certain scorchroaches lurked within. He knew it only took a sliver of sunlight to ignite a barbecue.

With the door opened, the Cruiser pulled inside and parked. Sunshine spilled into the man cave without result. Mr. Havlock climbed out and emerged from the garage, spruced up as he could be in a clean white tank top, open button-down plaid shirt, and brown slacks.

He grinned wickedly at Grandma Anna, Cab, and Murray. "What the hell are all of you staring at? Next time I'll rip your goddamn houses out of the ground!"

Cab grabbed Grandma Anna's sleeve and muttered, "Let it go. We've had enough confrontations today."

Mr. Havlock chortled as the garage door whirred shut.

Grandma Anna shook her head, dropped her arms, and wrung her hands. "I swear to God I'm going to kill that man."

Cab placed his hand on her back. "You and everybody else."

Murray looked longingly at the bike. Maybe now he could hop back on it and pedal like mad to the brambles. Even though the neighbors had distracted Grandma Anna for the time being, he knew she would soon be turning her attention his way.

Cab regarded Murray, noticing he had inched closer to the porch. "Save the bike ride for tomorrow, son. Runnin' from our problems ain't gonna fix 'em."

Grandma Anna sighed and looked Murray up and down. "Now that the busybodies are gone, I'd like to see what's in your pockets."

Murray reluctantly stepped onto the walk, distancing himself from the bike. He reached into his pants pocket and showed Grandma Anna the letter opener and box of tacks. "Just these."

"And those." She pointed to the scissors at Murray's feet. He nodded and picked them up. "I'm pretty sure you're not doing an art project out here."

As much as Murray dreaded retelling the story, he knew it was the only way to reach out to help the boy. If he was grounded for it, then so be it, but he hoped Grandma Anna or Cab would believe him.

He took a deep breath and exhaled through his nose. "I used the scissors to pry open Missus Vitikin's window. Then I tried to help the boy out of her basement, but he was too scared to leave. So I left him there. He told me Missus Vitikin isn't his grandma; he didn't know who she was. I swear it's the truth. I swear."

Cab shook his head. "It's too weird of a story to be a lie. Though we still need to see for ourselves."

Grandma Anna held out her hand. Murray handed over the office supplies. "Agreed."

"I just don't get why she'd be kidnappin' kids. Especially since there's one next door to her."

"Let's not jump to conclusions. I still need to see this child." She noted Murray's reaction, his mouth opening in retort. "I'm not saying I don't believe you, Murray. We need to be rational and have physical evidence before we hurl accusations."

"Your grandmother's right. I got a feelin' these women have been conspirin', so if one of 'em is hidin' a kid, you know damn well the rest of 'em know about it."

"So… What do we do?"

"Go about our lives like nothin' odd is goin' on. And then put a pot of coffee on for me this evening. I'll mosey on over about ten, and we'll see if the freaks come out at night."

⬟ ⬟ ⬟

The hour arrived, and the bell rang punctually. Murray answered the door in his *Punisher* T-shirt and black sweatpants.

Cab smiled, his baggy eyes twinkling. He was similarly clad in dark colors: black slacks, charcoal-gray pullover, and chocolate loafers. "You look like you're dressed for bed, son."

Grandma Anna appeared behind Murray. "He is, and that's exactly where he's headed. Say goodnight, Murray." Murray grumbled and headed upstairs. "I'll be up there in a second."

Murray lingered on the landing for a listen.

Cab shut the front door. "So far the block's quiet. Everybody's lights are on, though, and that worries me. After this afternoon, you can guarantee there'll be mischief."

"That's what I'm afraid of. Killing my garden was the last straw, and now talk of a poor child being locked up right under my nose..."

"Believe me, I'd call the cops if Eveleth wasn't mailin' 'em cookies every month."

"Cookies?"

"That's what Mable Jarret tells me. Her son took the deputy job there 'bout a year ago. So we're gonna have to be creative to get 'em wavin' a search warrant."

Grandma Anna nodded, mulling for a moment. "There's a pot of coffee on in the kitchen. Grab yourself a cup. I'm going to put Murray to bed."

She headed upstairs to Murray's bedroom. He was snuggled beneath the comforter, wrapped up like a cocoon, as if he'd been there the entire time. An unseasonable chill sliced the night air, the windows frosted along the frames.

Murray managed a half-smile, still disappointed at being unable to stay up later. "Are you and Cab gonna figure out how to stop the witches?"

"The witches?" Grandma Anna sighed. "Listen, sweetie, I

doubt they're witches, but they're certainly acting erratically. Now, enough crazy talk, at least until Cab and I get to the bottom of the things. Don't worry yourself about it, okay? You're safe here."

She kissed Murray on the forehead and left him to ponder in the cold darkness. Relief washed over him. Grandma Anna believed him after all, more or less. He was glad Grandma Anna and Cab had his back. He still couldn't help but wonder if his mother possessed the same gift. And if not, what made him so special? How had he ever become immune to fire? And why would the witches want him for that? It wasn't going to stop them from being burned at the stake, if that even happened nowadays.

Murray recalled the undertaker's remark.

Witch hunters. To this day, they burn them at the stake and dump them over these bluffs.

There would be a full moon soon. Why that mattered, who knew? Maybe the witches were going to summon a giant scorchroach to blow up the whole town. Or maybe they sacrificed gifted kids to a pack of werewolves. The comic books were talking again. Murray already witnessed magic firsthand; that horrid necklace had cast some sort of sleep spell on him. This entertained another thought. The young witch with the sleight of hand, impossibly turning an apple into a rose. Where had she gone, and how did she fit into the equation? She seemed too young to be part of the terrible trio. But on the same token, outside of the cellar window, she had bossed around Mrs. Vitikin.

Murray dwelt on her princess-like looks as he drifted off to sleep.

Murray's eyes snapped open at the sound of the doorbell. He looked at the clock. 10:30 p.m. on the dot. His heart thumped as worry overcame him. One of the neighbors was making a house call, and he bet his Marvel collection it was a witch. He hoped Cab was still visiting with Grandma Anna. At least then his paranoia would ease.

He sat up and crawled out of bed. He hurried over to the window facing the boulevard, ducked down, and cracked it open. He peered over the sill like a soldier in a foxhole. Ms. Crestwick, clad in a black, long-sleeve evening gown, waited on the doorstep. The front door opened, and the exchange drifted on the biting breeze.

"Good evening, Anna. I hope I didn't wake you."

"Of course not, Claret. Is something wrong?"

"I just wanted to apologize for this afternoon."

"It was a misunderstanding, that's all. It's not the first, and certainly won't be the last."

"That's not what I wanted to apologize for."

"Oh?"

"May I come in?" She withdrew a crystal decanter from her dress. "I thought maybe we could discuss it over a glass of wine."

Murray went into panic mode. If inviting a witch into the house was anything like a devil, the foundation would be turned upside-down. He ran across the room and cracked open the door. He sneaked into the hall and tiptoed to the landing. He did not know if Cab was still around, but he couldn't take any chances. There existed a high probability a neighbor in their midst would try something after hours. Of course, he still needed to sketch a Plan A. Once again, his impulsiveness led the way. He lingered at the corner, five steps from the staircase, out of sight but within earshot.

Cab cleared his throat. "Hello, Claret. What brings you over at this hour?"

Ms. Crestwick paused, surprised. "Good evening, Cab. I could ask you the same. Care to share a Merlot with us?"

"I got coffee. It keeps me on my toes."

"Does that mean the burglar's up, or is he fast asleep?"

"Could be in your house for all we know."

Grandma Anna shut the front door. "Claret wanted to speak to us about this afternoon."

Ms. Crestwick sighed. "Well, just you really, but since you're both here…"

"Let's have a seat in the kitchen. I'll get us some glasses."

Murray peeked around the corner. Cab trailed behind Ms. Crestwick and Grandma Anna. He glanced up at the landing, winked at Murray, and entered the kitchen. Murray slowly descended the staircase, step by step, gritting his teeth at the slightest creak. He reached the foyer and held his breath, listening.

The front door opened. Mrs. Muldoon crossed the threshold, grinning wickedly, her hair tame, straightened to the small of her back. Like Ms. Crestwick, she donned a black evening gown as if attending a gothic ball. She held a rusted key in her right hand and, upon realization, pocketed it. Though only an inch taller than Murray, her presence seemed colossal.

She reached within a dress fold and revealed the gnarled necklace of dead roots and leaves. She shook it teasingly. "I'd say this matches your shirt."

Murray knew the rosary all too well. Recollections of its strangulation attempt sent a shiver down his spine. He back-pedaled until his heels hit the stairs. Mrs. Muldoon approached him, clutching the necklace with both hands like a steering wheel.

A thump and a clatter came from the kitchen, sounding as if a chair toppled over, followed by shouts from Cab and Ms. Crestwick. Murray and Mrs. Muldoon glanced down the hall, momentarily distracted. Murray spotted his opportunity and acted on impulse. He lunged past Crazy Daisy and reached around the door jamb. He felt for the bell, found it after a second, and pressed it repeatedly like an impatient Trick-or-Treater. He had no idea if it would work, but he hoped it would grab Grandma Anna and Cab's attention.

Mrs. Muldoon pulled the rosary over Murray's head and down around his neck, then yanked him back into the house. The twined roots constricted at the touch of skin as she withdrew her key, raised it, and willed the front door to shut. The stench of tar slithered up Murray's nostrils. His head clouded and eyes glazed. He lost his footing and plopped down on the bottom step, wrenching at the necklace to no avail.

Grandma Anna staggered into the hallway, colliding back and forth with the walls as if inebriated. She locked gazes with Murray and collapsed face first, unconscious.

Another crash from the kitchen and glass shattered. Murray gagged, unable to swallow, fighting off the sleep spell weighing down his eyelids. His fingers turned purple, struggling in a one-sided tug-of-war.

Mrs. Muldoon chuckled. "Quite the spitfire. Let go; get your forty winks."

Murray stared down the hall through flitting eyes. Cab rounded the kitchen corner and sprinted toward Mrs. Muldoon. He cocked his fist back and slammed it into her face. Blood sprayed as the blow lifted her off her feet; she landed hard on the foyer floor.

Murray's head swirled. Sleep tugged at him like an anchor.

Cab placed his hands on Murray's jaw and tapped him on the cheek. "C'mon, son! Stay with me!"

Murray felt his consciousness sinking, his vision like a rowboat in a hurricane, on the verge of capsizing at any second. He squinted, battling the blur, straining to focus. Mrs. Muldoon lay on her back, out cold, blood gushing from her nose.

Grandma Anna was sprawled in a similar position, face first, still. Cab drew back his hands, straightened, and looked over his shoulder. Ms. Crestwick stormed down the hall, dress flapping behind her.

Murray's eyes closed, opened for a split-second, then shut and fluttered.

Ms. Crestwick stopped short, held out her hand, and displayed the empty decanter. "I think Anna and the boy would agree… It's well past your bedtime, Mister Linlith."

Cab massaged his knuckles and made a fist, ready to re-use it. "Take another step and you'll be eatin' hardwood like Daisy."

Murray gained a moment of clarity, like someone snatching their last breath before drowning. His vision focused and zoomed in on Ms. Crestwick's hand. The ring. She wore an emerald ring. He recalled the pretty young woman outside the cellar window. The apple transforming into a rose.

Ms. Crestwick pulled the decanter's stopper. The newel post cap unscrewed and shot into the ceiling, exploding into splinters. Cab ducked as sawdust rained down. He rubbed his eyes, briefly blinded.

The emerald ring glinted. A miniature nebula—like pollen and pixie dust—encircled the decanter. The blood-red cordial materialized within and bubbled up to the brim. Ms. Crestwick tipped the vessel sideways. The sleep potion streamed out like from a fire hose. It hit Cab straight in the mouth, his lips still parted in surprise, and gushed down his throat as he stumbled back and flailed. He tripped over Mrs. Muldoon's unconscious body and fell beside her, instantly sound asleep.

Ms. Crestwick smiled and pocketed the decanter. Murray's eyes closed, his mind whisked away to a red brick silo beneath a full moon.

Chapter 9

Murray came to with a pounding headache. He blinked his tired eyes. The blurriness fluctuated as he took in his surroundings. The smell seemed familiar, reminiscent of an old baby blanket. Murray's vision focused. The blue-green vinyl interior jarred him. He was slouched in the backseat of Cab's Cadillac. The rosary was gone, and his hands were bound behind his back. He wriggled onto his right shoulder. His brow knitted. The boy from Mrs. Vitikin's basement sat beside him. He bounced excitedly, grinning from ear to ear. He looked at Murray and placed his index finger to his lips.

The driver's side door opened, and Mrs. Vitikin plopped inside. She turned around and scowled, like a mother sick of her children bickering. "You should have stayed asleep, boy. It would have saved you some pain."

Murray wriggled, attempting to free his wrists. "Where are you taking me? And why is *he* here?"

"You both have something we need. Now shut up, or it'll be nap time!"

"But everybody's gonna see him! And yesterday you were calling me a liar!"

Mrs. Vitikin backhanded Murray across the face. "Shut up!"

The boy giggled. Mrs. Vitikin faced forward and backed the car down the drive. Murray massaged his face as tears spilled down his cheeks. Evil Eveleth's admission jostled in his brain like wet clothes in a dryer. They had something they needed, which only meant one thing: the boy possessed an immunity to fire as well. But why would the witches want that? So they couldn't be burned at the stake? Murray had yet to see a mob of people with torches. And how would they even take someone's gift from them?

The car stopped. The passenger's side door opened, and Mrs. Muldoon climbed in. Her swollen nose still seeped blood while the center of her face had turned black-and-blue. She slammed the door and stared straight ahead in silence.

Mrs. Vitikin eased the car down the boulevard. "Anna and Linlith?"

Mrs. Muldoon smirked. "Anna's tied up on Havlock's doorstep behind the tree. I peeked in his basement window earlier, and the scorchroaches had multiplied. All he needs to do is turn a light on. Claret has Linlith in her trunk."

"Perfect."

Mrs. Vitikin stopped at the end of the block as Ms. Crestwick's Sunfire backed out of her driveway.

The jovial boy leaned toward Murray and whispered, "Soon our time will come."

Murray craned his neck to see out the rear window. Ms. Crestwick pulled up to their bumper. The block beyond was dark, save for three street lamps.

And then lights started to switch on in Mr. Havlock's house. Mrs. Vitikin and Ms. Crestwick noticed as well, for they were fixated on the rearview mirrors. The windows lit up across, diagonal, and down like an odd version of *Connect Four*.

Mrs. Vitikin and Ms. Crestwick floored the cars to the next block while Murray gazed at Havlock's house. A basement light blinked, and the house exploded, rocking the block like a broken gas main. The windows shattered and breathed fire. Flames leaped through the roof. A fireball obliterated the garage door, crossed the street, and burned out on Cab's driveway, leaving a fiery trail. The trees reduced to smoldering, blackened skeletons as the grass became littered with campfires.

Murray hollered. "*Grandma! No!*"

Mrs. Vitikin backhanded Murray without taking her eyes off the road. "She's dead! Dead like your mother! Now get over it!"

Murray sank into the corner of the backseat. Tears spilled to his chin, and his head somersaulted. Not Grandma Anna. Why her? The one person who had taken him in after he had lost everything. Gone. Just like that. And now he had no one. He clutched his stomach as the heartache spread like a virus. It made no difference to him if he lived or died anymore. If he was to be sacrificed, then so be it. He sobbed uncontrollably, all the while wishing it was all a bad dream.

One block later, the Cadillac curb-checked and parked. Evil Eveleth and Crazy Daisy stepped out and slammed their doors. Murray knew they needed to act fast. After the explosion, the police and fire departments were surely on their way. If only evidence existed of the arson. Unfortunately, Grandma Anna's body on the doorstep would look suspicious. There would be no way of proving the witches had brewed the firestorm.

Murray looked out his window. They were parked at the Fennely Farm, a few yards from the rotted worm fence. In the distance sat the charred foundation, which Murray now understood to be another result of pyromania. To the left stood the red brick silo, the focal point of his rosary nightmare.

The boy pointed out Murray's window, his hands oddly unbound, as if not captive and merely along for the ride. Murray noticed his glowing tattoo, and it all made sense. His eyes twinkled, wide, entranced. "That's our destiny. With our gift, they will have a greater power. And we will live in the shadow of a god."

Murray shoved the boy back in his seat. "Wake up! You're being sacrificed, too! Are you that stupid? They're killing both of us, idiot! Both of us! Just like they killed my grandma! All so they can't be burned by hunters!"

The back doors opened. Mrs. Muldoon grabbed the boy. Mrs. Vitikin yanked Murray outside by his bindings. The air smelled thick of smolder, undoubtedly from Havlock's house. The moon shone bright on the roadside like a streetlamp. Ms. Crestwick's Sunfire sat behind the Cadillac. The trunk popped open. Cab thrashed inside, surrounded by blood-stained roadkill, his wrists and ankles tied with rope.

He locked gazes with Murray and relief flashed in his eyes. "Untie me, goddamn it! And let those boys go! I'm the one you've been itchin' to kill for years!"

The young woman in the sleeveless white dress appeared out of nowhere and rounded the Sunfire's rear bumper. Murray's jaw slackened. The sight of the witch surprised him, stunned by her beauty amongst the wrinkled hags.

Cab sized her up, taken aback as well. "Who the hell are you?"

The emerald ring caught Murray's eye. "Miz Crestwick."

Mrs. Vitikin squeezed Murray's bindings, causing them to cut into his skin. "Mind your tongue or I'll rip it out!"

The young woman bowed her head, her locks cascading

like a stage curtain, and turned her back on Cab. She whipped her hair back. Though Murray expected it, the revelation startled him. The woman now had Ms. Crestwick's face, but the rest of her youthful body remained.

She approached Murray and reached for him with her ringed hand. She touched the white *Punisher* logo on his shirt. It turned red and bled from its eye sockets. "My powers are far stronger than anyone's in this circle." She jabbed his chest. "Next time you speak, *that* will be your skull."

Murray bit his lip, wanting more than ever to scream for help, but they were blocks from civilization. For now, he knew he needed to listen. Although when the opportunity presented itself—and he hoped it would—he'd only be hearing his conscience yelling to retaliate and run like hell. He grimaced as the blood dripped from his shirt onto his shoes.

Cab rocked back and forth in the trunk. "Get your hands off him, witch!"

A pair of high beam headlights rounded the street corner, revealing everyone in the moonlit darkness.

Ms. Crestwick's face reversed in age a good thirty-five years, and she spun on her heels. "Eveleth! The shawl!"

Mrs. Vitikin threw Murray aside into a sandbur patch. He yelped as she removed her shawl and shook it out like a matador. A gray cloud that first appeared to be dust, but flashed and faded to navy blue, unfurled down the road. It expanded and extended across the land in a thunderstorm manner, sparking with electricity. The wicked magic jostled the car as it approached. Eyes wide, Murray watched as it passed by. With the driver sound asleep, snoring on the dashboard, the station wagon veered off the road, jumped the curb, and slammed head-on into a tree. The horn blared incessantly.

Mrs. Vitikin made her rounds and shook the shawl in every direction. The ethereal blanket covered the town, flashing with lightning, casting the citizens into an unforeseen slumber. Those already asleep never suspected a thing. Murray pictured police cars and fire trucks careening off the bluffs or piling up on a side street. Now they were really in a predicament, with no one to help but themselves.

Mrs. Vitikin retracted her shawl like a shade and placed it back around her neck. She raised the whistle to her lips, faced the wrecked car, and blew. The horn's tune changed from a tornado siren to a sonata, filling the accident scene with violins and clarinets.

Ms. Crestwick pointed toward the farm. "Bring them! Now!"

Mrs. Muldoon nodded and nudged the boy through the crabgrass. He walked willingly, hopping excitedly over the fallen fence.

Cab kicked his bound feet at the backseat, barely budging it. "Murray! Run! Get out of here, son!"

Murray staggered, wincing, covered head to toe in sandburs.

Ms. Crestwick clapped her hands, and the Sunfire's trunk slammed shut, stifling Cab's shouts. She snapped her fingers, and the wrecked car horn's symphony changed. "Ahh, Handel's *Messiah*. Much more fitting, wouldn't you agree?"

Mrs. Vitikin swung her cane and cracked Murray behind the knees. He fell to the ground before he could make his escape. He gritted his teeth. His legs felt bruised back to front. He crawled toward the fence. No matter the strange boy's excitement to die, he refused to let the witches have their way. He knew the kid's tattoo surged with mind control.

Mrs. Vitikin kicked Murray in the stomach. He gasped, tears brimming, and fought off the urge to vomit. He inched forward, eyes locked on the fence. If he could grab one of the fallen crossbeams, maybe he could shove it onto Mrs. Vitikin's legs and buy some time. The sandburs dug into his skin like a bed of nails. He struggled within a foot of the fence. He reached out.

Mrs. Vitikin loomed over him. She smashed his hand into the sandburs with her cane and ground his knuckles as if stamping out a cigarette butt. She reached down and seized him by the nape.

She jerked him to his feet by the bindings and held him tight. "You want to slither like a snake? I ought to shove a rat down your throat! Now walk, or I'll shatter your kneecaps!"

Murray obeyed, tripping over the tumbledown worm fence. Mrs. Vitikin refused to let him fall; instead, she shoved him forward, her hand on his back like a puppeteer. He stared at the towering silo, transfixed. The steel doors swung open, and swarms of scorchroaches scuttled from within. Each burst like a cherry bomb as it crossed into the moonlight.

Murray's stomach twisted, and a shiver racked his body. The reality of his situation struck home. Held captive. Grandma Anna dead. Cab locked in a trunk. No one could stop the witches from a midnight sacrifice.

Murray struggled to think positive. No more children deserved to die. They were going to escape this madness. Somehow.

Murray stumbled onto a gravel path, crunching at first what he thought to be rocks but realized he was trampling scorchroaches. He eyed the silo's brickwork. Constructed by the Devil's mason, each brick interlocked into the shape of a pitchfork. A thick, warm haze emanated from the doorway, creating a shimmer reminiscent of highway heat. A stench overpowered the breeze: blood, but not of one person or animal, of many.

Mrs. Vitikin dragged Murray across the threshold. His gut lurched as the copper scent filled his mouth and nostrils.

He gazed at the silo's tight confines. Three flashlights shone toward the roof. To the right of the doors, a dirt nest of scorch-roaches, the last of which scurried off into the night. In the center sat a triangular well, its walls made of vertical mirrors reflecting darkness from all angles. From within the hole, as if in a planter, an overgrown blackened willow tree reached to the roof. Various animal skulls hung from its upper branches, the lowest bough decorated Christmas-like with dead black cats dangling by their tails, dripping blood from their mouths.

Mrs. Muldoon emerged from the shadows holding a rotted dog's head. Murray's eyes widened even more in fright. It wasn't just any dog; it was Pontius.

Mrs. Vitikin spun Murray around, seized him by the collar, and lifted him into the air over the well. She dropped her cane and used her free hand to wind a willow branch through his bindings. She let him go, and he dropped a good six inches. He held his breath as he swung over the black hole, wanting to scream and thrash, but reluctant to move a muscle for fear he would plunge into the pit.

Ms. Crestwick entered the silo, still an old face on a young body. She pointed at Mrs. Muldoon. "The offering!"

Mrs. Muldoon tossed the dog's head into the well, missing Murray's feet by inches. He listened intently but never heard it hit bottom. Anxiety flowed through his veins. He felt he might pass out from fear alone. He tried not to look down, knowing it would only terrify him more. He gazed across the way, trembling, his brain bubbling with impossible escape plans.

Ms. Crestwick approached the well, reached up into the tree, and snapped off a horned animal skull as if it were a piece of fruit. It shivered in her hand, levitated over to Murray, and settled onto his head. The stench of rot spoiled his stomach, but he swallowed it down. The eye sockets were lemon-sized, large enough for him to still see out of, whether he wanted to or not. Again he yearned to kick and wriggle, yet he relented, glimpsing himself mirrored in darkness.

Across the way, the boy jumped up and down near the breeding grounds, his tattoo blinking like a radio tower. "Me first! Me first!"

Mrs. Vitikin and Mrs. Muldoon flanked Ms. Crestwick as they stood against the brick wall between Murray and the boy. Ms. Crestwick thrust her arms into the air, glaring at the rusted roof. The other two witches bowed their heads and clasped their hands in silent prayer.

Ms. Crestwick's young facade faded: the white dress stained black, her hair streaked silver, and her skin wrinkled prune-like. "Moloch, Habetrot! Morrigan, Tantalus!"

A guttural moan rose from the well, reverberating the bricks and loosening the mortar. The mirrored walls cracked. A hot, putrid stench of death, as if from the bowels of Hell, blew forth, rustling the willow violently. Leaves rained down, and skulls snapped off, tumbling into the growing darkness below.

Murray lurched, trembling. His branch creaked, swaying. Grateful Ms. Crestwick tied him to one of the strongest ten-drils, he was surprised he still hung, though whatever the witches called upon might eat him whole.

He looked at the boy, who was beaming and clapping like Santa Claus was coming to town. The dirt floor swirled into a mini-tornado.

A moan of a thousand dying men rocked the silo. The willow shed more leaves. Murray clenched his teeth, quiver-ing uncontrollably.

Ms. Crestwick advanced on the dust storm, sneering.

The boy's head cast a red halo. "Thank you for choosing me."

Ms. Crestwick swiped her arm through the tornado and backhanded the boy. His body fell backward, hit the ground, and then plummeted into the well. He screamed all the way down until a thunderous roar erupted. The mirrored walls shattered. The remaining leaves and skulls shook from the willow. Murray's branch cracked, dangling by sinews. The silo's bricks shifted.

Ms. Crestwick stepped within the tornadic circle. "Moloch, Habetrot! Morrigan, Tantalus!"

Murray knew it was now or never. If he waited any longer, he would be the next sacrifice. Soon his branch would snap and he would plunge into the well.

The rancid breath gasped from below, the push Murray needed. He fought off his nausea as his branch swung. He pulled his legs up into a fetal position, mimicking a wrecking ball. He tried to swing out, and as he did, the willow's tendril broke, and he caught air. He hit the ground a foot past the lip of the well and rolled into the wall. His animal mask cracked in half and toppled off.

Cab barged through the swinging doors with a curved dagger in hand. His face wrought with worry, it eased upon seeing Murray alive and well, then reddened with rage as he laid eyes on Mrs. Vitikin and Mrs. Muldoon.

Murray managed a half-smile. "Cab!"

Cab nodded at Ms. Crestwick. "Crazy witch keeps knives in her car."

He lunged at the utter of his last word. Daisy withdrew a handful of red rose petals from her pocket and threw them. They transformed into leeches flying at Cab. He batted them down with his arm and buried the blade in Daisy's side. She cried out as he retracted it and shoved her hard. She shrieked as she fell over the edge, into the swirling darkness of the well.

A centralized earthquake rattled the silo. Roars and snarls like a sleuth of grizzlies bounced off the walls. Bricks tumbled down. Maggots seeped between the stones of the well.

Cab pointed the dagger at Murray, blood trickling off the blade. "Stay there, son! I've got this in two shakes!"

Mrs. Vitikin sneered. "Make that one."

Cab charged Mrs. Vitikin. Her cane morphed into a black mamba she swung like a machete, hoping to sink its fangs into Cab's throat. He dodged the attack and shouldered her like a quarterback. He landed on top of her, his dagger driving into her sternum. She wheezed and flailed her arms, attempting a counterattack, but instead lost her breath as the snake slithered off. Cab wrenched the blade free and got to his feet, gasping.

Ms. Crestwick was oblivious to the goings-on, her face upturned, arms shaking in the air like a belly dancer's. Her hands writhed, fingers elongating and curling, bathed in black light. "*Moloch, Habetrot! Morrigan, Tantalus!*"

Murray rubbed his bindings vigorously against the bricks. Ms. Crestwick needed to be stopped before there was no turning back.

Murray and Cab jumped as a pillar of blood and fire shot from the well. Flames coursed up the willow's trunk and branches to the canopy. The roof of the silo blew off, revealing the full moon.

Cab charged Ms. Crestwick and kicked her in the back. She stumbled, lost her footing, and toppled into the well. She managed to snag the lip and dangled from the edge, blood showering her, flames singeing her clothes. Her grip slipped as she tried to dig her nails in deeper. Her face and body transformed into the young woman. Her soft eyes twinkled.

She smiled weakly. "I'll leave town tonight. You have my word. Please. Help me."

Cab crouched, his head glistening with sweat. "You'll be leavin' alright."

He sliced with the dagger like he was drawing a line in the dirt. Ms. Crestwick screamed, her body aging as she fell into the witching well, leaving four fingers behind.

Murray's bindings broke, and he yanked them off his wrists. He ran to Cab's side. They gazed at the well. The pillar of blood and fire extinguished, the well seemingly satiated, but the burning willow remained. The tree swayed violently, slamming back and forth into the silo walls. Bricks and flames rained down from everywhere.

Cab and Murray shielded their heads. A green glint distracted Murray for a split second. He spotted Ms. Crestwick's dismembered finger sporting the emerald ring. He reached down and scooped it up. The ring slid off easily into his hand. For a moment he had a crazy thought the jewelry might give him magical powers, like in *The Hobbit*. And then he thought better of it and tossed it into the well where it belonged.

The bloody dagger seemed to be Cab's new pointer finger. He gestured toward the battered doors. "Make tracks, son! Now! Go, go!"

They both dashed across the silo. The walls collapsed around them, bricks and flames hitting the dirt, booming like cannonballs. The willow split in two from the surrounding chaos and bridged the well, which glowed ultraviolet, feeding on the ring. Murray and Cab stopped running a good distance from the wreckage and caught their breath, gazing at the piles of smoldering bricks.

The Fennely Farm burned down once again and buried the well for good.

⬠ ⬠ ⬠

Murray looked up at Cab. "Do you think everyone's still under the sleep spell?"

"Let's hope they are. It'll give us time to turn heel. We'd be lookin' pretty guilty if the cops showed up right about now. C'mon."

Murray followed Cab to the road. The Sunfire and Cadillac sat along the curb, unscathed. The Sunfire's passenger side door was wide open, the backseat laying in the front, serving as Cab's escape hatch. The wrecked car across the way was silent, the horn's orchestra in intermission.

Murray and Cab climbed into the Cadillac. The keys dangled from the ignition. Cab revved the engine, pulled away, and whipped a U-turn. They left the farm and slowly headed down the side roads. When they turned onto Blossom Boulevard, the extensive damage had them stunned. The trees were torches, the canopies aflame, leaves falling like volcanic ash. Every house on the block burned, the structures blackened skeletons, unsalvageable and inextinguishable. Clearly, the explosion caught like dominoes or scorchroaches scuttled aplenty. Grandma Anna's house was an inferno, Grandpa Macon finally laid to rest.

Tears spilled as Murray thought of Grandma Anna. He had no one left to love him, care for him, and remind him of his mother. That life was all gone now, like Windom, reduced to ashes and memories.

Cab reached over and squeezed Murray's knee and shook it. "I'm sorry, son. It's just you and me for right now. Hope that's fine with you."

Murray dried his eyes, nodded, and managed a smile. "Yeah. That's fine with me."

Epilogue

"Murray? Hurry up or you'll be late for school!"

He put the finishing touch on his latest painting and sighed. Though five months had passed since the ordeal in Windom, he was finally starting to fall into a daily routine and feel at home. There were no prying next-door neighbors, exploding insects, or absence of children. In fact, he made friends with the boy across the street, who was a year older. Normalcy took root, and he hoped it would remain.

He stepped back and regarded the artwork. The red brick silo stood beneath a sunny sky in a field of roses, not far from the blue farmhouse. It was how Murray wanted to remember it. Now all the witchcraft business seemed like a nightmare, surreal, an impossible occurrence. He set down the brush, grabbed his backpack, and walked away from the easel.

"Hold on, Mister!"

Murray stopped in his tracks. Now what? Did he get paint on his school clothes? He would be late for sure. He turned as he slung the JanSport over his shoulder.

Aunt Eva's eyes narrowed, hands on her hips. "What did you have for breakfast?"

"A Pop-Tart."

"*Fine.*"

While Aunt Eva had been in and out of his life, Murray was glad she had assumed guardianship. She was kind, loving and, above all, concerned for his well-being. She always asked about his day, and they even took weekend trips to state parks. While he yearned to see the serenity of Superior, he wanted to stay as far away from Windom as possible.

Aunt Eva followed him to the entryway. "Do you have all your homework?"

Murray sighed as he laced his tennis shoes. "Yes. And my history paper."

"And don't forget, I want to buy you a new shirt for the wedding."

"I know."

A horn honked twice outside.

Aunt Eva smiled. "I know you know. Have a good day at school, sweetie."

Murray was too slow to dodge a kiss as he stood. "I will."

He said goodbye and stepped outside. The day felt cool and crisp, a warning winter loomed on the horizon.

The horn honked two more times.

Murray shook his head and grinned. Cab chuckled behind the wheel of the Cadillac. Wanting to maintain their friendship, he moved a few miles away into a senior living complex. He said he was sick of neighborhoods and all the strenuous yard work. In other words, he finally came to terms with his age, as young as he behaved.

Murray climbed into the passenger seat. "Is that really necessary?"

Cab laughed. "I just like to see the look on your face, son. What took you so long? I almost grew my hair back."

"I was painting."

"I figured, but it's not worth a tardy. What were you workin' on this time?"

"The silo."

"That pile of bricks?"

"Yeah, but with roses and a blue sky. Happy thoughts, right?"

"Happy thoughts, yes siree."

Murray gazed out the window as the Cadillac backed down the driveway. While the police asked a few questions about the "Windom Fires," they never put their finger on a suspect. Instead, they chalked it up to a wildfire, being the middle of summer and all.

Cab slapped Murray's knee. "So what are you doin' this Saturday?"

Murray rolled his eyes. "What do you think?"

"Watchin' me get *married!* Son, I can't wait to settle down, let me tell you. I was gettin' too old to be single."

"You're still gonna pick me up for school every day, right?"

"I'm not startin' a full-time job, son. Just writin' a new chapter in life."

"Good. 'Cause I hate taking the bus."

"Well, then maybe I should buy you a new bike."

Murray raised his brow. "I think I forgot how to ride one."

Cab laughed. "My boy, you never forget."

Murray smiled and watched the neighborhood turn to storefront windows. As always, Cab was right. He would never forget his mother, Grandma Anna, and the unusual gift he had.

Most of all, he would never forget the witching well.

ABOUT THE AUTHOR

Over the last two years S.D. Hintz has published two novels, a novella, and five short stories. He is the former Editor-in-Chief of KHP Publishers and extremely active on social media. He currently lives in northern Minnesota with his wife and 2 children.

**Press
Presents**

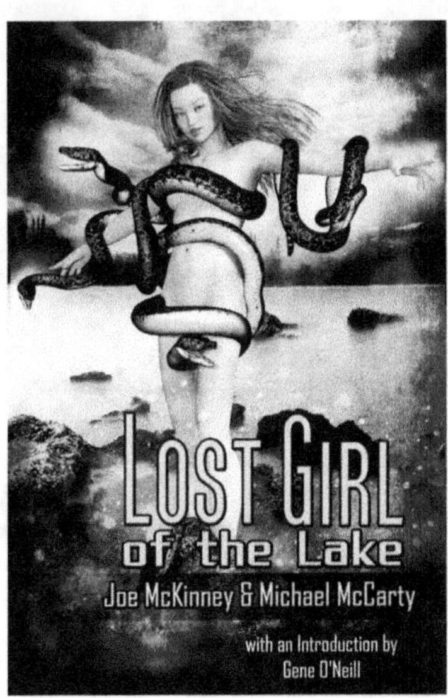

Lake Livingston: August, 1961

Mark Gaitlin is 15, the son of one of the wealthiest men in Texas, and on the most boring summer vacation of his life. His days are filled with the pomp and circumstance of country club life, while his nights are a parade of one embarrassment after another at the hands of giggling teenage girls.

But the piney woods above Lake Livingston are dark at night, and they hold many secrets for an impressionable youngster on the cusp of becoming a man. And one night, after skinny dipping in the lake with a mysterious local girl, Mark Gaitlin's life takes a crazy turn into the fire and brimstone religion of backwoods snake handlers and abandoned villages haunted by old family secrets. If he can survive the snakes and the ghosts and his own family's dark history, he just might make it out of the woods alive.

And something else...he just might become a man.